To Ashton
Thank You

Three Lies

A Novel

By

Kent Hughes

Mike Parker, Editor

D1508639

Imprint Books

Charleston, South Carolina

Copyright © 2005 Kent Hughes

ISBN: 10
14196-2130-09

DEDICATION

I dedicate this book to my parents,
Jesse and Maiseville Hughes.
When I became a man, I realized just how important you
both were in my coming of age.
I thank God for the deck that you placed in my hand.

TABLE OF CONTENTS

ACKNOWLEDGMENTS

First, I would like to thank God for blessing me with the courage to change the things I can, the patience to endure the things I can't change, and the wisdom to know the difference.

With all sincerity I would like to thank the readers and supporters of my first novel, *4th Sunday in the Dirty*. Because of you I was able to buckle down and complete *Three Lies*.

Believe me, it felt so good to hear you ask, "Kent, when is the next book coming out?"

It's now my biggest reason to write.

Again, I would like thank Mike Parker for believing in my work and showing me that true friendship is only a phone call away.

To my family: Tamaia, Chasity, Kenesha, Michael, Phillip, granddaughter Harmony and my best friend ever, my love, my wife Tiffnii Hughes. Oh! And I can't forget my sweet Mother-in-law Louise Pulley. To my parents Masieville and Jesse Hughes(RIP) and my sisters and brothers, Theresa, Jesse Jr, Elevese, Jannifer, Sheila and Sherick and all my in-laws' nieces and nephews...I love you humans!

My thanks go out to the old nursing staff at Dobbs Youth Development Center: Mary Jo Harrison, Sonya Pickens, Bridgett Williamson, and Verna Bouie ... my dream team.

Thanks to, Rev. Dr Freddie Barnes, Jeanne Williams, Tracy Walker Wright, Prinn Deavens, Michael Garrett, LaShawnda Keys and all of the co-workers that supported me. I know you couldn't believe it at first, but *Three Lies* will make you more of a believer.

Technical Supporters: Thanks Mike Parker, Sandra Parker, Lydia Parker, Tiffnii Hughes and Tiffany Chanease Stancil, who graciously proofread the manuscript.

.

Preface

If you are a fan of stories of mystery and mystique and involving downright deception covered with a rich layer of distinct love, honor, dedication, justice, and redemption (and aren't we all), then *Three Lies* should meet and exceed your literary needs. *Three Lies* draws readers into the deceiving and dynamic world of the Johnson family through the tragic-comic soul of Donnie Jackie Johnson. Through prose and poetry, Donnie chronicles his family history, a history that has led him to the seat on death row. Donnie describes the visions of his cousin Beany Harold, a young woman with a sixth sense that *4th Sunday* fans will remember well. Beany's visions of blue birds and words "cripple cries make dancing lies" haunt Donnie throughout the book. Beany and a certain person in a dripping wet raincoat are enough to bring most readers occasional chills.

The Johnson boys – Donnie, Maurice, and David – grew up in murky waters themselves to a single-mother and stepfather whose relationship created the perfect ingredients for child abuse and neglect. Psychiatrists, psychologists, social workers, and education researchers conclude today that child abuse and neglect can actually be enough of a stimulus to alter negatively the brain chemistry of developing youth. Donnie and his brothers were no exceptions to this research finding. David is distant, Maurice is a hauntingly insecure child psychologist, and Donnie is an inmate on death row sentenced for the murders of three women – accused, but how guilty is he, if he is guilty at all? That is up to you to decide, and this book will keep you working on that decision from cover to cover. Donnie Johnson, the main character, twists the common and exaggerated story of a "bad" family rendering a "bad" child in a manner that pulls and pushes readers to ask deeper questions about the extent to which Donnie represents the "perfect victim."

Author Kent Hughes blends an acute authenticity with a dramatic flair of folklore and fiction to draw the reader into this book. Characters and their experiences are portrayed with poignant details. The Johnson family story, although fictional, is plausible largely because the author draws from his decade of experiences as an infantryman and drill sergeant in the United States Army and the transition into civilian life with various jobs in Juvenile and adult corrections.

Mr. Hughes began writing poetry, short stories, and songs as a grade school student. He initially set out several years ago to write a book of poetry. The way he tells it, an acquaintance offered a bleak outlook that "most poetry books don't reach most readers, unless the author is already famous." Given that his poetry was an initial spark and inspiration for him, it is understandable that the author was disappointed. It is even plausible that he would have ceased efforts to pursue his hope.

Instead of retreating, the former soldier remained steadfast to his own vision by creating an innovative and exciting genre he calls a "noveltry." Similar to his first pass titled *4th Sunday in the Dirty*, this book is a unique blend of narrative and poems, of the essentials of novels and poetry telling a story and building a plot, climax, and conclusion in a refreshing, fluid, and complete fashion.

His work is the embodiment of his creed: "To inspire one child, if not all, to follow him into a world where everything can be exactly the way you want it to be … if you capture your imagination and bind it in your own book."

This book speaks to my work in Foundations of Education, which include three wings, Theory and Social Foundations of Education, Research and Measurement, and Educational Psychology. My colleagues and I focus on social justice and the holistic well-being of students and their families. I find much transferable information in this book to enhance the teaching, research, and service aspects of my career. Although, I have a minor in English from the University of North Carolina at Wilmington (only four courses short of a double-major) where I read fiction relentlessly, my current position as a professor of Social Foundations of Education leaves little time in my life to read the fiction books I might enjoy. Time, however, was not a factor in reading this book of fiction, this noveltry, because the story grabbed me and wouldn't let go! It was as gripping to me as a book that most of you will recognize, titled *Donnie Brasco*. So, set back and enjoy the ride that is **THREE LIES**.

From the author:

→ poem: if we do not release
the chains of trauma
we were burdened w/ as
kids we never grow
out of them

Chains Still on Child

Tested by time
An evolution of dreams
Castaways depart …
On silent beams
By daylight …
Shine
By night …
Unseen
No future, yet told
Only death it seems

Deep beneath the halls of pains
Link together by balls and chains
Tremendous …
Spirit
Nothing to gain
Only sad memories
Of guilt and shame

Called upon
By mercy and grace
The heels of dawn …
Were soon replaced …
By trembling hills …that
Devoured old faces
Now …
Our secrets rest …
Within these places
Hidden behind my secret smiles
My future …
Untold …
Chains still on child

1

KENT O' HUGHES

Three Lies

THREE LIES

CHAPTER 1
— DR 12-32

Donnie

Sitting in the corner of his slightly damp cell, his mind started to cave in like someone had vice grips attached to the top of his head, pulling him away from himself.

The cell must have been a hundred years old. The smell of death managed to stick to the painted and repainted walls. Notches engraved on the walls were called deadlines … lines left by the unknown soldiers before him. At the end of the last cluster of marks were teardrops signifying the last day they would spend on earth before the state of North Carolina took their lives.

The dim lights in his cell only gave enough rays to help identify his body during count. The smell of death covered the room like a mildewed old blanket. Sometimes the guards would leave the food trap open to let the smell die thin. One cup of urine slung out of the trap would end that little comforting moment.

Between the hate he inflicted on himself and preparations the state of North Carolina conducted on behalf of his departure; his existence became merely a state of being. He had gotten used to being alone, but the cries that echoed from the dead men walking past his cell during an occasional execution made him question his own mortality.

He hurt so badly inside, but for all the selfish reasons a convicted murderer would hurt.

Donnie Jackie Johnson had been a celebrated and highly decorated soldier. He spent ten years in the United States Army and was planning to make it a career … until the secrets buried in his dark past resurfaced and rewrote the last chapter of his life before he had time to turn his next page.

"You feel like eating, boy," the correction officer, or CO as they called them, mumbled, as if not to care if Donnie ate again … ever. The guards hated working at Elizabeth City State Prison. Working on death row didn't make things any better.

Sometimes Donnie would go days without a toilet flush. The guards were too lazy to cut on the water. All it took was for one of the inmates to flood a room and the stench of urine and feces would become unbearable. When the guards got sick of the odor, they would finally turn on the water.

Camden was considered one of the poorest counties in North Carolina and jobs were few. Working at the prison was considered good pay. Although the prison was clean, the attitudes were nasty … both guards and inmates.

If you wanted to see how societies would react if freedom was inaccessible, all you had to do was commit a crime … a crime that carried a life-or-death sentence, and you would see the dingy grinds of a madmen spore.

Donnie or DR12-32, which stood for death row inmate number twelve thirty-two, tried to slip as far away as he could from his cell. In his solemn moments he would write anything that would come to mind.

When he was in the military, he would write poetry to his lady friends or for the other guys in his unit to send to their girlfriends.

Sometimes he would write in grim detail about the victims who had suffered his wrath. Writing about this subject was a way to hate himself and understand that his death was entirely necessary.

An Outer Body Redemption, he called it.

With so much time on his hands and not much else to do, Donnie decided to write his life story hoping the world would understand why he told those three damned lies.

Donnie heard the metal taps of the CO's patent leather shoes as he came walking down the highly waxed hallways.

"Eating time, you, people!" the officer yelled loudly. It was breakfast time and if you didn't get up, you didn't eat. The morning was the best chance of getting anything you needed for that day.

"Excuse me, sir, can I get a pencil and two sheets of paper?" Donnie asked the officer politely.

"What? You're not getting ready to write that book this early, are you, DR12-32?" the guard asked. "You trying to write a best seller or something?"

"I've got only a little time left," Donnie explained. "I don't want to leave without finishing my book." The officer gave Don the usual three-inch pencil and two sheets of paper. Donnie thanked the officer and went to his makeshift desk, a toilet made into a seat, and a cardboard box he used as a table.

The hardest part for him to write was the beginning. He wasn't sure where it all began but he did remember when the pain started. In his dedication he thanked everyone who inspired him to write his first and last book, ***Three Damned Lies.***

****

Three Damned Lies
By
Donnie Jackie Johnson

****

*

Acknowledgements

First, I would like to thank my sorry, look-the-other-way, and turn-the-other-cheek, getting-your-butt-kicked-by-my-stepfather ... mother ... Stacy Johnson. Thanks to you, Maurice, David, and me repeatedly got molested by your stupid husband that you insisted on us calling, "Daddy."

I'd like to thank the juvenile court system for giving me a place to stay and food to eat while I learned to fight, steal, cheat, and ask for toilet paper. Even more, thanks for trying to save my life.

To Mrs. Westly, thanks for telling me I wasn't going to be nothing. You were right.

To all those families whose lives I destroyed: Sorry. I was mad at the world, so I swung at the wind.

Donnie Jackie Johnson

I was three years old when it started.

It was nothing for my stepfather to come in after a hard day's work and start going off.

"Stacy, I know you had something to cook besides corned beef hash for dinner," he would yell, furious. "Here I am working twelve-hour shifts and come home to this."

Mom would try to explain to him how she bought only what she had enough money to buy. James Earl didn't want to hear that. He would rather blame everything on us. He would often tell her if she didn't have us, how better off he and my mother would be. The sad part about it was, she never argued this point. As a matter of fact, she had the nerve often to agree with him. If he didn't try to kill us one day, I believe she would have.

One reason he never had enough money was because he was on crack cocaine. He would leave for days, usually on Friday, coming back on Sunday to recover for work.

Hanging out at Robin's Soda Shop, which was a far cry from a soda shop, was his spot. The soda shop sold ice cream to the kids in the front of the store and drugs to the addicts in the back. It seemed like every few days, or so, I would ride with Mama to pick his stupid tail up. He'd come dragging his sorry self out back of the shop, looking like he didn't know who we were.

That was the one-time Mama could talk smack to him and he had nothing to say ... but the worst was yet to come.

When he got home, comfortable, and down off the high, the foolishness would start.

He would be on the couch watching the hunting channel until he fell asleep. Somehow, he would forget where he and my mother slept because unconsciously, he found his way to my brother David's room. All we could hear was a muffled cry from David.

We would see my stepfather coming out of the room, putting his belt on, staggering, and breathing all hard. David would be in the room crying, saying how he was going to kill that son of a bitch one day.

David was the oldest of the boys, so he had a room by himself. He claimed he needed his privacy. I think he was forced because my stepfather had a thing for pre-teen boys.

That went on for a couple of years until David was old enough to leave home. He promised that he would never let anything like that happen to us.

Until ... one night, when David was about sixteen years old, my stepfather went into his room and came out with a busted nose and blood dripping from everywhere. I knew it would be the last time I was going to see my older brother. I was right. My stepfather called the police, pressed charges, and sent him off to juvenile home for boys. He knew David wasn't going to say anything about what had been taking place because David didn't want his manhood questioned. What was so bad about the whole situation was that before David left home, he told Mama what was going on ... and she did nothing about it.

Soon after it would be my turn. At twelve I had already decided. I was not going out like a punk. And I was going to keep my promise to my little brother that nothing and no one was going to harm him.

Sometimes, James Earl would come in the room Maurice shared with me and say things to me like: "Boy, you are getting too big to be sleeping in here with that boy. You need to get yourself in that room your older brother had."

I was so mad at him for running David away from me; I wasn't even scared of him anymore.

One morning I was too sick to go to school. I had a fever of about one hundred and ten or something. Mama gave me medicine, cooked chicken soup and told me I could stay home from school. She told me to stay in bed and, if I needed something, call her at The Gas Mart.

It was on a Monday and James Earl hadn't been seen in about three or four days. I was lying in bed watching the show Cops on TV when I heard someone banging on the door. I figured it was James Earl and didn't bother to open it. He must have lost his key because it was as if he was trying to break the door down.

A few minutes later the door swung open, and he came in talking loudly. After a while I could hear him fumbling around in the kitchen. I laid there quietly, hoping he didn't detect that I was home.

I always kept a small bat in my room to protect myself from him.

***

Donnie had been writing for about three hours now, and time had passed quickly. In some ways, that was a good thing, but in a more sinister way, the time that passed only brought him closer to the end of his existence.

As he placed the two sheets of paper into the folder and stored it under his bunk, he heard keys rattling from a distance.

The CO came up to Donnie's door, using the biggest brass key on the ring, opened the flap, and placed something that looked like dog food on a plate inside the cell.

Something was a little different with this corrections officer. He spoke with a faded voice as if to be ... maybe, scared even.

"Hey, sir, are you alright in there," he whispered, a little nervousness edging his words.

Before Donnie answered, he peeped out the little flap to see exactly who it was. Standing in the hallway was a fresh, scared-to-death ... boy. He could not have been any more than twenty-one years old.

"What's your name?" Donnie asked. The boy paused.

"Stanley Miles, sir," he replied, reluctantly.

A brief wave of concern swept across Donnie. The CO seemed so young, so out of place.

"What the hell are you doing in a place like this?" Donnie asked. The boy seemed to understand the concern that lay at the heart of the question.

"I needed the job, sir," he said. He quickly shut the food flap and rushed off to the next inmate.

Since the new CO was fresh meat and Donnie was on his last leg anyway, Donnie figured he'd live his last months trying to make amends with someone. The new officer would be the one.

Each time Officer Miles worked on the dead hall, as the CO's called the unit, Miles would spend time talking with Donnie on an array of subjects. As the days went by, Donnie got so used to talking to Officer Miles that whenever Officer Miles was off duty would he never say anything to anyone. He would just sit at his desk and write.

***

James Earl finally made his way into my bedroom. I was waiting for him. Knowing what he might try, I made sure to put all my clothes on early. Just in case.

"Boy! What is your sorry behind doing in bed? You need to be at school," he said, like he was my daddy and ... like he cared.

"I was feeling bad, and Mama said I could stay in here today."

"See, that's what's wrong with you kids. Y'all got ya'll's Mama fooled, but you can't fool

13

me, boy. Get your lazy tail out that bed," he said, pulling the covers off me, hoping I didn't have any clothes on. I surprised him, though, because I broke that bat out and began to beat on his head like I was Barry Bonds, and he was a baseball.

I ran out of the house and left him for dead. I ran all the way over to where my mother worked and told her what happened.

Instead of her worrying about me, she got on the phone and called the police. James Earl pressed charges and I was sentenced to three years in a juvenile youth facility.

While I stayed in the Camden County Detention Center waiting for placement, all I could think of was Maurice and what he had to face with my sick stepfather around.

Being that I was in lock up, there wasn't too much time for feeling sorry for myself because guys would try to take advantage of you if you showed any kind of weakness. Most of the time, I would just stay off to myself and wrote home to my brother. Just as sure as my name is Donnie, that sick sadistic beast made his way to my little brother's room.

Maurice came to visit me at Grangers Youth Center, a training school for juvenile boys. He told me that James Earl came into his room and nearly knocked him unconscious and commenced to raping him repeatedly.

Just as David had done earlier, Maurice kept his mouth shut and didn't tell anyone.

I'm thinking either he was too scared, or he was worried about his manhood being taken from him as well.

All I could say as I cried profusely on the inside, "I'll kill that you-know-what when I get out of here. I should have made sure he was dead the day I beat him with that bat."

Maurice smiled and said with sure confidence, "He'll get what is coming to him soon enough."

"Why?" I said. "What do you have in mind?"

"I bought me a gun from Terry, that drug dealer from school."

"And?"

"And I'm going to blow his brains out."

I was all for that, but there was one or two little problems. First, Maurice didn't have the guts to kill anyone. Second, I didn't want to see him in my position.

I was dying to get out of training school, and I learned quickly that the only way to get out when your time was up ... was to go with the program.

There was this one counselor named Mrs. Bruttersworth. She always seemed to have all the right answers. Behind her back we used to call her "Pancake" because she was big as a house and ass flat as a pancake, all she need was butter. She was a great person and help guide me right out the door. She always gave good advice and reminded me that if I left here and didn't learn anything, it would be because I didn't want to learn.

Training school probably saved my life at the time. But it took one more stop before I could make it back home to freedom. My court counselor, Mr. Peterson, and my social worker, Ms. Jeanne

Mosey, thought I might need to spend time in a group home before going back to live with my mama. They said that I needed a little transitional period to work my way back into a regular home setting.

Me, I didn't see anything regular about my home, so actually I fitted in good with my family without the practice run.

The one good thing that came out of my situation at the time was the fact that I was able to work on getting my high school equivalency diploma. I even tried to find my religion by taking religious courses, which in the long run helped me find myself.

***

"As I call out your name, state whether you are living or dead," the CO said before the last body count was made. "DR12-32."

"Dead, sir."

"DR 11-25."

"Dead, sir."

"DR 10-36 … DR 10-36," he called again, hyper-extending his voice. The officer rushed down to look inside Thomas' cell. All you could here was the CO yelling over the radio for help.

"I guess the poor fellow couldn't wait for his due date," Donnie thought to himself.

Donnie considered himself to be strong. He said from the beginning, he was going to make the state kill him if it was the last thing he did.

CHAPTER 2
Mama Who?

"Donnie."

"Yes, sir."

"You have a visitor at the glass," Officer Miles said with a smile.

"Me? A visitor? Who is it?"

"It's a preacher."

"I'm getting dressed. I'll be ready in a second," Donnie said as he rushed to put on his clothes. Donnie knew he would have to go through the routine of putting on enough leg irons, handcuffs, and shackles to hold down a two-ton elephant. But since it was his first visit other than those from his lawyers in almost four years, he was kind of curious to see who it was.

After he got ready, the officers came in with their routine, and it was off to the visitor's area.

As Donnie turned the corner, he saw it was Rev. Tavone McKnight. After seeing who it was, he knew something had to be wrong.

The officers assisted him to his seat, locked the loose chains to the floor, and all but one officer stepped out. Rev. McKnight picked up the phone provided for him and then nodded for Donnie to pick up.

"How are you doing, man?" the reverend said.

"Doing fine, Rev. How about yourself?"

"I can't call it, man."

17

Donnie had known Rev. McKnight from the little league baseball team. Donnie would take his little brother Maurice out to practice at times, and while Donnie was standing around, he would often talk with Tavone. Tavone would sometimes go and pick both Donnie and Maurice up and take them to church with him. After Donnie got in that trouble with his stepfather, they kind of lost contact.

"So, what brings you here? How's Alex, T.P., and those two girls of yours? Have you seen any ghosts lately?" Donnie asked than started laughing.

"Everyone's fine," Tavone replied, skipping the last question, and going back to the first one.

"I'm here on behalf of your mother."

"My mother?" Donnie asked. "What about my mother? Did she get locked up again?"

"No … I'm afraid it's a little worse this time." Tavone paused for a moment, trying to figure out exactly how to tell him without getting too emotional himself. "Your mother passed away last night."

"How?" Donnie asked with little expression of sorrow.

"She overdosed on heroin."

"Where did they find her this time? Lying outside on the street?"

"No. She was still at Winslow Homes. They found her in the bathroom face down in the toilet. The coroner said she passed out …drowned, according to the autopsy."

"The one good thing about it," Tavone said, "at least your brother Maurice had visited her the day before she died."

***

[Mama Who?

Stacy Who?

Maurice and I would stick together like glue at this point. Wherever I went, he would not be too far behind.

I was now seventeen years old and felt as though I was a grown man. I worked out daily at the gym, keeping my body in shape, maybe secretly preparing for that final conflict with James Earl.

I could tell I made him sick because he said nothing to me, and I said nothing to him.

Poor Mama lost her job and she depended solely on him for any type of support. This meant she caught pure hell. I didn't really feel sorry for her because of the stuff she allowed him to do to us. I wanted so bad to ask her why she let this happen. Why did she just turn her head the other way? I couldn't figure it out. What did matter was if he ever tried anything again, he would be a dead man.

Being that Mama couldn't give us any money for anything and the people in Camden all knew me and knew about the little accident, there was no way I was going to get a job. I did what any teenage boy would do. I sold drugs. I was a little scared at first because I didn't want to end back up in juvenile court.

I started off just selling weed for Terry. After I got my little clientele built up, I eased into selling crack cocaine for some of the older guys. Every now and then I would see my stepfather hanging around trying to get some crack on credit and using my name for collateral. I would tell the boys if he got anything and didn't pay to kick his ass because I didn't like him. He wasn't a total fool because he would pay every payday. I actually ended up giving money to my mama to help buy food or to get her a pack of cigarettes.

After a while, Mama started missing.

The word on the street was she was ... out there ... way out there. Some of my so-called drug-dealing partners were getting little sexual favors from her for crack. At first, I didn't want to believe it until one day I was in this part of town called the Alley.

She was in the back seat of our car with two younger guys known to be drug dealers. Her head bobbing up and down as my stepfather stood there like he was on look out. I figured he finally drug her down with him. All I could do was turn my back and walk away. I'd rather people think I didn't know, or I didn't believe it than to go up to the car making a big scene.

I think that was when I lost all hope for me ever getting a full deck to play life's crazy game. I didn't get to know my father, my mother was on crack and selling herself, and my stepfather was so messed up it wasn't funny.

I guess all that's left for me to do was to kill him, but in some ways, I felt like he was already dead.

I started to spend more time concentrating on Maurice and trying to help him have at least a little clarity in his direction. Sometimes when I went to pick him up from baseball practice, I'd sit and talk to Rev. McKnight for hours. It's like he knew what was going on without me really telling him. His son T.P, Mrs. Harold's boy Alex, and Rev. McKnight's stepson Jason seemed good for Maurice. They never judged him on anything, but his playing ball and he was good.

Once in a while Rev. McKnight would let Maurice spend the weekend with him. A couple of times I would even hang out with them, but I had to get back out there and make that money.

For a while everything was going pretty good. The crack heads went their way, and I managed to pull Maurice and myself the other. I knew I was going to face the demons of reality soon. Satan's son did not let me down.

I guess James Earl felt like I had a little too much power for my own good. He didn't care that I was bigger than Maurice and David were. Maybe trying to show me who was in charge of the household, he came into my room one night holding the same bat that I beat his butt with when I was younger. He caught me off guard and started beating me in my back while I was sleeping. He hit me so hard that after a while I couldn't feel a thing. What really messed me up was when he started to pull my pants off and began to rape me.

21

Being that I hung with Rev. McKnight, I had a little knowledge of how God worked because I managed to muster up enough strength to reach under the mattress, get my silver .45 and squeeze off a few rounds. I pushed him off me and left him for dead ... again.

Crawling, and in unbearable pain, I barely made it into the living room where I could get to the phone. I called 911 and told them what happened as they kept me on the line. I was trying to talk until I began to have back spasms and began to cough up blood from all the blows. I thought he was dead but that fool came out of the room all bloody, telling me how I was going to pay for this.

The operator heard every word he was saying and told me not to shoot him anymore if he didn't come near me.

I think he forgot one little thing. I wasn't Maurice or David, and I was going to tell everything.

When the paramedics arrived, I was sitting in the sofa and my stepfather was lying on the floor bleeding to death.

When the police got on the scene, it was time for poor old James Earl to put on his act. He started to yell out how I was trying to kill him and telling them I had a gun.

Of course, because I had been in trouble so many times and my name was all over the precinct, they rushed to judgment.

I was always known for talking trash to the police and never showing any fear, but this particular night I said nothing. All I could do was concentrate on putting James Earl in jail or in his grave.

When we got to the hospital, escorted by police, we were both sent to the emergency room for treatment. As soon as the doctor asked me what happened, I asked for a rape kit and explained that my stepfather had been raping my two brothers nearly all their lives and tried to rape me over the years. I told them that he had been on drugs and everything. This is one time that I wasn't going to care if the whole world knew what I was going through with this sick monster. He was going to do some time, or I was going to find a way to take him out of his misery.

August 17th, a day I'll never forget, was the court date. Here I'm a young innocent 17-year-old boy and Stacy ... my so-called mother, was sitting in the courtroom with me. All she worried about was if my stepfather was going to jail or not. I guess he had beat her behind so much that he had beat the sense out of her.

"I wonder what they had been feeding James Earl in that jail," she said. "He looks all fat and plump."

Now I'm thinking to myself, "Here she is giving a rat's ass about what he looks like and I'm sitting here hoping this fool don't get out of this like he seems to get out of everything else."

He had already been charged with all kinds of stuff – taking indecent liberties with a minor, first-degree rape, and some other stuff that I didn't know or even wanted to think about.

Mama really kind of pissed me off because she was crying and hollering all through the trial. The trial didn't last but two days because we were dirt poor and his lawyer seemed as though to want James Earl in prison just as much as I did.

James Earl knew that he had got a bum deal when he found out his court appointed lawyer was Willie THE LOSER Peterson. In Camden, although everybody went their own way, when something like this was found out to be true, there was no need for even having trial. The town's people had already found James Earl guilty. It was a matter of how much time they were going to give him. The jury took only about thirty minutes to come back with his verdict. I knew that he was going to do some time, and I couldn't wait. I couldn't wait to see the look on his face when they sentenced him.

When they asked him to rise, he had to get help from his wacko lawyer to even stand. The judge started reading off all the counts and the time that ran with them. When it was all over, James Earl was to spend about sixty-five years in prison. Mama started crying and passing out like she was at Ma Elsie's funeral. What I couldn't understand was how she forgot so easy how he had messed up her children's lives. If it weren't for him, maybe we would have had a little more normal of a life.

When the bailiff walked him out of the court, James Earl turned and yelled out to me:

"This will be you someday, and you can bet your sweet ass on that."

I just gave him the finger and, with a smirk on my face said, "Long as I'm not in the same cell with you." The courtroom was packed because this was big stuff around here.

So little happens that this was even better than watching the O.J. Simpson trial.

Everyone was all ears, so I put on a little show and said.

"As long as it's you first, I gives ... not a damn." I threw up my hood sign and started asking anyone that would listen: "Did you get what you were here for?" Most just shook their heads, as if to feel sorry for the family. My older cousin, Beatrice Harold, just walked over to me and said, "Don't worry, Donnie. These people love a good show. I'm going to try to get you back in school or into Albemarle Community College. I heard they have a program that can help you get the high school equivalency diploma. Then maybe you can get into Elizabeth City State, my old alma mater, even if I have to pay for it myself."

Beatrice was a very sweet lady. You could depend on her for anything. People around town wondered where she got so much money from because she often would stop by some of the poorer people's houses in the neighborhood and take a light bill or something and just pay it for them. She would never give out money unless you were a kid and she saw you in the store or something. My brother wanted to be her son instead of his own mom's. I even wanted to be her son sometimes. Her daddy and my real daddy were brothers. Her daddy was a lot older than mine. She was a lot older than me and didn't seem like a cousin ... more like an aunt.

I told her thanks and knew she would keep her promise.

She told me to go and see Mama, saying that Mama needed me right now.

"Mama who? She ain't my mother. I don't know who she is anymore."

"Look Donnie, I know your mother doesn't seem to have her head on straight right now, but it's kind of up to you to help keep your family together. And I promise to help as much as I can."

I took on the role of father and son, as well as family doctor. When Mama would get drunk, she would pass out right in front of Maurice and me. Pretty soon it came to the point Mama was more like a sick older sister than a mother. I had to find a way to get her some help before I would be thanking people for their condolences.

I called Beatrice to see if she could help put Mama into a drug treatment place. There was a good one in Goldsboro, North Carolina. She agreed, and now it was up to Stacy, as I now called her, to agree. The funny thing was, she agreed. Like all parents that are in situations like this, she knew how screwed up she was.

Beatrice came over one day to help Stacy pack her clothes, but it was about an hour or so too late. Stacy was out the door and nowhere to be found. As soon as Beatrice called her to tell her that she would be over, she jetted out the door like Arrow Smith. I didn't even see her leave. I thought she was in her room getting her stuff together, but she had slipped out the back door like a crackhead at a drug bust.

Beatrice and I drove to every hot spot from Camden to Elizabeth City trying to find her, but she was nowhere in sight. Finally, we gave up and went back to her house. Beatrice insisted that Maurice and I stay over until we could find her, which seemed to be fine with Alex and Maurice. Maurice stayed over there all the time anyway.

Beatrice was nice and all, and she knew a little of what was going on with us because of this noise lady named Lucy Gray. As much stuff as she'd come and tell my mama about Beatrice's business, I knew she ran back and told her what she thought was going on in our family. My guess was that she added to what was already in the newspapers.

When we spent the night, Beatrice would make sure Beany and Alex slept in the room with her. Beany, I could understand, but Alex was thirteen, and I think he was a little too big to be sleeping with his mother. I guess when you're a marked man, even family members take shots at you, even if they don't mean to. Maurice and I were just glad someone was interested in us enough to take out time with us.

Beany seemed like the only one that genuinely didn't mind we were there. The problem was Maurice, and I was scared to death of Beany. One night she found her way into our room, which was actually her room. She was standing at the door with a black raincoat on, dripping wet like it was raining inside the room.

She then said with an angelic like voice:

"Donnie, when you start to see the blue birds at your window, that means you are going to

be freed. They're only there to watch over you. Don't be scared. Don't be afraid. They all remember when you took care of them. When you go home, everything will be all right. Just don't make the birds cry. Never make the blue birds cry. When you are alone, you are never alone. You were born in sin with a good heart, a heart that will allow you to enter."

Beany turned around and walked out of the room. For a long time, I would stay awake every night so frightened I had to keep the light on. I didn't know what she was talking about. Most of the time no one did, until something bad ended up happening. I never saw any blue birds, and we couldn't find Mama either.

For the next two days we searched everywhere we could think of short of driving to the Virginia state line looking for her.

After a while Beatrice just said, "Let her go. Maybe after a while she will find her way back."

I'm thinking to myself, "Maybe I'll get lucky, and she will show up dead." I don't know if I really meant that, but it seemed like it would fix everything, at least for the moment.

Just like Beatrice promised she helped get me into The College of the Albemarle. Because she helped out so much, I decided I would make her proud of me.

The first thing I did was think about what Ms. Buttersworth always warned me about when I was in training school – my so-called friends. I stopped hanging out late nights and started being totally committed to my studies. I even started running track for the school team. I was getting noticed by some of the major schools in the area.

Then one day out of nowhere Mama shows up at Cousin Beatrice's door looking like she had just been through a car wash. She was asking for money and for food.

"Girl!" Beatrice said, frowning like she was riding by the Jennings turkey farm on a hot summer's day. "Where in the world have you been? Come on in here and let me run you a bath. You smell like something crawled up in you and died. Now this just makes no sense. As soon as you shower and I feed you, we are going for some help."

Mama was so out of it that she didn't have the strength to fight back.

"Boy!" Beatrice said, "Go warm up some food for your mama."

"Mama who? She ain't my mama," I said again, but in such a low tone that even a blind man that knew Kung Fu couldn't hear me.

While I was in the kitchen, I heard Beatrice on the phone asking someone to come over to help with Mama. I figured it was either Teeny Baby or Rev. McKnight. I'm thinking that Rev. McKnight lived too far, so it had to be Teeny Baby.

Man! I was hoping it was Teeny Baby. She was the prettiest lady in town. I think every man in town had their turn with her, but she had to go marry that ugly Mr. Cefuss before I could get my turn. I was way too young for her taste, but if she had just held out for a little while longer, I know I could have got some action.

29

She was really a sweet lady and was crazy about Beatrice. I figured after Mama sobered up, she would start to act up and Teeny Baby would be there to have Beatrice's back. From what I heard Teeny Baby could beat anybody in town. I don't know how true it was, but they say she beat up these two fat ladies at the same time and actually had them running.

Mama looked like a new woman when she came to the kitchen table. She was still out of it but at least she looked human.

"What are you looking at boy? Got some kind of eye problem? All of this is your fault. Since you think you are so much of a man, we'll find out how much of a man you are when I put you out of my house."

I didn't say anything because as far as I was concerned, she was talking to herself. At this point, all she had was herself because I didn't give a crap about her. If it wasn't for Beatrice, she would probably be locked up or dead by now.

***

While James Earl was locked up awaiting trial, Beatrice would come around bringing food and making sure the lights, water and stuff like that was in order. Mama was trying to hang in there at the time, but drugs were kicking her behind.

One thing about Beatrice, she never gave Mama one single dime and never asked for anything in return. Beatrice just did as much as she could to help her.

***

Mama sat trying to pick a fight with me, but soon Beatrice came in.

"Stacy, when you finish eating, get those bags I packed for you in the room. It's time for you to get some help before you kill yourself or something."

Mama didn't say anything. She got up and went to the room to get the bags Beatrice prepared for her. When Stacy came out of the room, Stacy must have thought she was going to run again ... but she was fooled this time. When she went talking and walking towards the door like she was going to run, the doorbell rang.

"Come on in, girl! Stacy was just starting to act the fool, and I'm all out of Oscars," Beatrice said as Teeny Baby walked through the door.

"Girl, you aren't going anywhere without me, are you?" Teeny Baby asked Mama as she stood with bags in hands. One thing about Teeny Baby, she would always be straightforward when it came to saying what was on her mind.

"Stacy, what happened to you? Looks like you've been sleeping with the enemy, and he beat your ass. Girl, you better get yourself some help. Not everyone has someone like Beatrice willing to help out."

Mama just broke down and started to cry. Then she turned and looked at me.

"I'm sorry," she said and walked out the door.

That was the last time I saw her for a long time.

Maurice and I were to stay with Beatrice until Mama returned from the drug treatment center. Beatrice would make special trips to Goldsboro to check on Mama, leaving me, Maurice, Alex and Beany with Teeny Baby and Jr. Ceffus. I was scared that one day Jr. Cefuss was going to come and catch me in bed with Teeny Baby. I know it was a schoolboy crush and that she wouldn't give me the time of day, but in my dreams, I was tearing it up every chance I got. Jr. Cefuss always kept a little eye on me.

One time when I was over there and overheard him.

"That boy is a little too big to be walking around in my house not doing anything," Jr. Ceffus said. "He needs to get a job, be a little more productive with himself."

At first, I thought he was being mean or caught me looking at Teeny Baby. After having a long talk with him, I found that he was an all-right guy. For the next year, Maurice and I bounced back and forth from Teeny Baby and Jr. Ceffus' home to Beatrice's house. I guess they were splitting the responsibilities of helping us out.

***

Rev. McKnight wasn't at all surprised by the reaction he received from Donnie after he told him about his mother.

"Donnie, if you would, let's just say a prayer together. Remember, she did bring you into this world," he said.

"Don't remind me of that. My existence seems more like a curse than anything," Donnie replied with a bitter cold voice. Rev. McKnight was about to speak when Donnie broke in.

"Ok! Ok! Whatever. Let's pray so I can go back to my cell. I'm getting tired all of a sudden."

While Tavone was praying, Donnie just sat there staring at his bald head, wondering who was getting the most out of the prayer, him or Tavone? He soon called for the guards, telling them he was ready to go. Rev. McKnight hung the phone up, waved good-bye to Donnie, and walked out.

Donnie waited as the guards unlocked the leg irons from the floor. He held his head down and maybe dragged his feet a little as he walked out of the room.

Once back in his cell, Donnie lifted his mattress and sorted through some pictures of his mother. He began to cry.

"Why, Mama? Why did you have to choose such a screwed-up life for us? Why couldn't you just pray and believe like the rest of the family? I hate you, Mama."

The hate he voiced against his mother was only the cry of selfishness, the selfishness that we all can feel. Selfishness born of the need to feel loved, born of desperate desire to belong.

As the dimness of his cell became blur and the tears refused to dissipate, Donnie sat and started to mourn his mother's death ... and his death to come. Hardly ever did he think much about what was to come, but when he did, his will to live was overpowered by his acceptance of death to come. Tonight, was going to be one of the several times Donnie cursed God and asked for forgiveness in the same breath. He balled his fists and placed them to his face. Sitting down as his elbows dug into his thighs and with his arms together holding up his head, Donnie cried until he could think of a reason not to.

CHAPTER 3
Mail Call

"How does it look outside?" Donnie asked Officer Miles.

"It's sunny, sir. Ain't a cloud in the sky. As a matter of fact, I saw a blue bird on the steps as I walked out my door this morning."

"Funny thing you said that. I used to feed them when I was a little boy. I found a nest of them in a tree, and I would dig for worms, smash them up a little and feed the chicks."

"Well, maybe that was one of its distant relatives wanting me to tell you thanks."

"I doubt that," said Donnie.

"Why do you say that sir?"

"I have done a lot for a lot of people and never heard thanks from anyone. A couple of 'atta-boys,' but no real thank you. People never say thanks in the real world. In the real world, all people want from you is – what they can get from you – and what they can take. Sometimes I feel like freedom isn't really free. We all pay a price at some point. I'm just paying my price to the world, the real world."

"Sir, you can be pretty deep when you want to be."

"Yeah, so can the ocean. I guess I'm so deep that I jumped into the deep end of the ocean and forgot that I couldn't swim. Now I'm drowning like a mutha."

"You know," Donnie broke in upon himself. "I want to understand something. Why do you call me 'sir'? Number one: I lost the right to be called 'sir' a long time ago, and number two, you look to be only a few years younger than I am."

"Well, sir, this is the way I see it: if you are paying your debt to society, then you are doing more than what a lot of people are doing. Some people go through life always holding out their hand like cups, wanting someone else to drop what they have worked hard for right into their hands. I've never seen you whining. You just pay your debt to society. That merits a 'sir' in my book."

Donnie took a big gasp of air.

"Boy! I have done some crying – it's just in the dark, cold dark tears."

Officer Miles made his rounds to talk with the other inmates, making his mandatory fifteen-minute checks. When he got back around to Donnie, Donnie had a book of poems that he had been working on for a while.

"What you got there, sir?" Officer Miles asked with a slight bit of curiosity.

"I have some poetry that I started writing on when I first got locked in this hell hole."

"Can I hear one of them."

"You sure, man?" Donnie started to flip through the pages trying to find one that he thought the officer would love to hear.

"Officer Miles, do you have a girl?"

"No," Officer Miles replied, "I don't have any children."

"No, I'm talking about a woman, a girlfriend," Donnie asked, laughing.

"Yes, I got a little sweetie pie."

"Well, I'll do one for you, and maybe you can even give it to her for her birthday or something."

Donnie was having little flashback of when he used to write poetry for his friends when he was in the military.

"Are you ready, Boss?" he said to Officer Miles.

"Ready as can be," the officer replied.

If Love Had Eyes

If love had eyes
It could see through and around me
It could see how I was lost
And how you found me
It could see the colors of my unchanging heart
It would see you … to me … And we would never part

If love had eyes
It would know how I feel
By the glow that shows
By the touch that's real
It would see us together and bond us as one
Each day would be new … like we've … only just begun

Understanding the magic, our love needs not to see

But, if your love had eyes, you'd see love in me

***

"You wrote that? No kidding," said Officer Miles in amazement.

"Yeah, I wrote that for someone years ago."

"I know she enjoyed that."

"Well, I wrote it for this dude."

"Whatever floats your boat," said Officer Miles with a burst of laughter.

"No, man, not like that. I used to write stuff for guys when I was in the army to give to their girlfriends or wives," Donnie explained.

"Well, that was pretty damn good."

"Thanks."

"Why don't y'all just kiss to make it official?" said one of the other inmates on the hall.

"Shut up, dead man. You know dead men can't talk."

They all started to laugh. Then they got silent once they thought about it – all except Officer Miles. Once everyone had stopped laughing, he continued as he walked down the hall.

"You guys are crazy," yelled the officer as he completed his shift and headed off the Dead Hall.

"Mail call!" the on-coming officer shouted with a tone of voice that conveyed his feeling of disgust that anyone would ever write to Donnie and the other pieces of scum on death row.

Donnie hadn't received a letter in more than a month, so he wasn't looking for any mail.

"DR 12 –32," the officer called to Donnie's surprise.

"Here, sir!" Donnie shouted. The letter was from David. He hadn't heard from David since he had been on death row, which was going on seven years.

***

You Got Mail

I was doing all I could to keep my grades up in school, hoping I could get a scholarship to run track at a big-time school.

But it just wasn't working out.

I needed a 2.6 grade average, but I was only getting by. Although I wasn't satisfied with my grades, Beatrice was very proud of me. On the night of my graduation, despite the small commencement ceremony, everyone I knew showed up.

David, Maurice, Alex, Beatrice, Teeny Baby, Jr Cefuss, Beany and my buddy, Rev. McKnight, were all seated in the front row. Mama even came.

I tried to act like I didn't care that she showed up, but deep down inside, I knew I wanted her to be there. When graduation was over Beatrice told me to come outside, saying she wanted to show me something. When I walked outside, she got behind me and put her hands over my face so that I couldn't see. I was wondering what was going on. When she removed her hands, everyone was standing by a car. My car. A blue and gray Ford Mustang GT 5.0, with sunroof T-top. It wasn't new but it was new to me. I was so happy, I had to blink back tears. That was the first time anyone had bought me something.

The first question I asked was why?

"I had to do something for you," she said, smiling. "You tried so hard, and you need something to drive to college."

I kind of figured I wasn't going to make it into any college with the kind of grades I had, not with a free ride anyway. I was counting on a track scholarship to get me through, but I just didn't cut the grade. I waited out the summer working at the Dollar Buck, a small discount store chain, unloading trucks and whatever they needed me to do. The manager, like everyone else in town, knew me from the trial and from being in training school, so she trusted me only to do the hard labor, rarely letting me work on the floor and never behind the cash registers.

Sometimes they would have us stocking the store at 12 midnight until about seven or eight in the morning. I had fun because that's where I met my first girlfriend, Thai Simmons.

I had a few girlfriends before I met her, but no one to actually call a real girlfriend. I was having so much trouble in school, I think the girls were actually scared of me. Since the fact was all over school that my stepfather raped me, some of the kids used to think I was gay. No one dared say it

40

in my face because I wouldn't have thought twice about beating someone's butt. I basically stayed to myself and looked out for Maurice.

Thai was from Raleigh, North Carolina, and didn't know anything about me. She had just moved here to attend Elizabeth City State. I knew I really liked her because whenever we were working at night, I would always find a reason to work close by her. If she needed anything, I would break my neck to get it for her.

One morning after we had finished stocking, she went outside to take the trash. I was the first out there to help her break down the boxes to put in the dumpsters.

"Why do I have the feeling that you are following me everywhere I go?" she said. "Are you stalking me?"

"Yes, I am," I answered, hoping she knew I was joking.

"Well, I like it," she said. "It makes me feel like someone is watching over me."

"I am watching over you ... all over you."

"What did you say?"

"I mean ... like to make sure you don't get hurt putting that stuff out. You know, you could break a leg or something climbing up and down those ladders."

"You could break your neck watching me climb up and down that ladder as well," she said, as if to have noticed me looking at her all the while and enjoying it.

I asked her if she would like to go out to breakfast after we got done here. Being that I was

41

so shy, my heart started beating fast anticipating her answer?

"No," she quickly said.

My heart stopped pounding and dropped to my stomach. I was sure that someone had told her a bunch of stuff about me, and she didn't want to go out with me.

She then quickly said, with the sexiest voice I had ever heard in my 18 years of living:

"Donnie, I think you are the finest and nicest guy I've met in a very long time, and when I go out to eat with you, I want to look real good for you. I want to make you want me real bad ... so bad that when we are served our food you will be already full off the whipped cream, cherry-smelling perfume I'll be wearing."

"Man!" I thought to myself, "I just wanted to eat. Now I'm ready to eat and go home to beat my troubles down."

I was definitely shocked by her response and happy she even considered giving me some.

All I wanted to do was eat breakfast.

"Cat got your tongue," she asked, picking a little.

"No. I just wasn't prepared for that answer."

"My man stays prepared."

"So, I'm your man now?"

"I think so. Don't you want to be?"

Being that I was a virgin, I was still able to hold my own.

Holding my own meant I was so scared I could have took off running like I was in my first track meet on the inside ... but Cool Hand Luke on the outside. And just to think, my first relationship with a true girlfriend all began standing by a dumpster.

We became inseparable. Everywhere you saw me, she was right by my side.

Mama was back in the house, and although I was old enough to be on my own, Maurice wasn't, so I stayed at home to make sure he had what he needed. I was more like the man of the house. I could do pretty much what I wanted.

Being that Thai was living in the dorms, she would come over and spend nights at a time with me, cooking and cleaning the house. It almost seemed like we were married.

Then the problems started.

School started, and I was off to North Carolina Central in Durham. With the money I saved from working and the money Beatrice gave me, I was able to pay tuition for the first semester.

I loved Thai so much that every weekend I would drive four and a half hours to see her. I was never too good at making friends, so I made it my business to come home every chance I got. The problem was Thai was an out-going girl and she had lots of friends, girls and guys. I could handle the girls, but I just could not understand why she needed guy friends.

One weekend I called to let her know that I was coming home, and she said that she was not going to be in town. The first thing I thought was she had another man. I started to question her every step. Then I started to wonder why she never came to Raleigh to visit me sometimes. She was from

Raleigh, but she never came this way. I thought that maybe when I was in Raleigh, she was with someone else. I had Maurice to start going around checking on her.

Then it happened. Maurice called me one night and told me that she was at a hotel with Andre Miller. What was so messed up about it was he was sixteen and she was twenty.

I didn't even think twice. I jumped in my car and drove as fast as I could to Elizabeth City to catch her.

When I got there, I saw the two of them and some other girl coming out of the hotel. I jumped out of my car, ran up, jerked her out of the car, and commenced to beating her. I didn't bother to ask any questions. All I knew was what I saw.

The guy and the other girl took off, not even waiting to see if she was ok. I made her get in the car and drove her back to my house, leaving her car at the hotel. She was crying and yelling so hard and loud that finally I stopped to listen to her as she held a handkerchief to her nose, trying to stop the bleeding.

"Why did you trip like that?" she said between sobs. "You know that I would never cheat on you. You fool, I love you."

"Well! What do you call being at a hotel with another man?"

"I call it helping a friend that was trying to get a room. All I did was help Yukon to get a room for her and her boyfriend. They were too young, so I just got the room for them. Who told you that I was at a hotel with someone else, anyway? You got

44

somebody spying on me now?" she asked, still crying.

"Yeah! I do have someone spying on you," I said.

"Why? Why would you do something that stupid? Have I given you a reason to do something like that? I tell you what, you don't have to worry about me anymore."

"Why?" I asked already knowing the answer.

"I think we need some time apart because I cannot be getting my ass beat like your step-father did to your mother. I am not your mother, and you damn sure ain't my daddy."

I began to cry, begging her to please forgive me, telling her I was sorry, promising her I would never hit her again. I promised to trust her.

She began to cry even harder, but only this time she was crying tears of sorrow. She agreed not break up with me and told me the next time I wanted to find out something about her, just ask her and she would tell me whatever I wanted to know.

I stopped the car in front of her driveway and started to hold her and began to cry on her shoulders. She always had a way of making me feel like I was someone.

Then she whispered in my ear.

"Let's go back to the hotel and get us a room. I got something I want to show you."

I almost broke my neck trying to turn the car around and head back to the Motel 6. Needless to say, she showed me things I'd never seen before.

The closer we became, the farther apart I became with my own family.

Maurice was doing his own thing in high school. He was a star player on the football and baseball teams. The whole time he excelled in school, Mama found herself falling in love with some man that ended up being just like the one the state helps me get rid of. Soon they were back to yelling and fighting.

One man, Percy, was considered a pimp back in his days. From the looks of him, pimping wasn't easy. Percy did have a job working with the county at the garbage dump. He would come home with a bunch of stuff that people in the neighborhood had thrown away, saying he was going to fix it up and sell it. Soon we had junk all over the place. Needless to say, neither Maurice nor I liked him. I think he could sense that we didn't because he never spoke to us, and we never spoke to him. He stayed out of our way, and we stayed out of his.

One night, I came home and saw that Mama's eye was all swollen. I asked her what happened.

"Baby, Mama's starting to lose it a little again," she said with a soft voice, trying to make me think maybe she didn't get her butt whipped.

"Is this fool hitting on you?" I asked, maybe concerned... a little. "If he is, I'll take care of him for you."

"No, I fell," she said.

All of a sudden, I had a flashback. Here she was taking up for another man, just like she had done for James Earl.

I quickly shut down like a nuclear plant with a leak, turned around, and went about my business. I could tell she was starting to backslide, and I was not going to get caught up in her web.

David called me one day and told me he had come across some money and asked if I needed any for school. I knew where it probably came from, but I needed it.

"If you got it, I need it," I said sharply.

I seemed to spend just as much money traveling back and forth as I did buying books for school.

Thai had moved into an apartment off campus with one other friend and began to ask for money all the time, as well. I started to feel like a bank, what with trying to come up with money for Maurice, helping Mama to keep the lights on, going to school, and supporting my lady.

I started back dealing drugs a little and thought I was smart enough to stay out of trouble. Being I was new in the area and the gangs in the Raleigh-Durham area were getting crazy, I thought I'd better get real and figure out another way that I could make a quick buck.

A few of the girls at the school danced at this club called The Play Pens. They would pay me to give them rides out there. They even tried to get me to come in to watch them perform, but I didn't like going in those types of places.

One day, Shanna, one of the girls that danced, told me I should try dancing sometime. I thought about it, but I couldn't imagine what would happen if some gay man came up throwing me money and me having to kill somebody, especially after going through that shit with my stepdad.

I was almost to the point of quitting school, when one day I was sitting outside of my dorm and Mr. Odom the mailman showed up.

"You got mail," he said as he always does.

Whoever had mail that day is supposed to say, "I got mail?" Then he could say, "You got mail." I guess he thought he was Spike Lee.

After going through his little ritual, he handed you the mail.

It was a letter from David. I ripped it open. The envelope contained a money order for fifteen hundred dollars and a note.

"Keep your head up" was all the note said.

For a minute I felt like I was on top of the world but when I figured out all the bills and the money I owed, I was right back where I'd started. I called Thai to let her know I had the money to help with the bills. She wasn't home so I left a message on her answering machine and headed back to Elizabeth City.

When I got home, I first stopped by Camden to check on Mama and to see if she was ok. I also wanted to make sure that Maurice was ok. Neither was home and I had no clue where they were. I went and picked up a few groceries and some kerosene for the heater. I didn't feel too much like driving back over to Elizabeth City, so I just chilled and waited for Thai to call.

It was getting late, and I hadn't heard from Thai yet. I finally got my stuff together and went to her house to wait there for a while. When I got there, a blue Honda Civic with Virginia license plates was parked in her driveway, and I could hear loud music playing. I figured she was home and some of her friends were over playing cards or something. I parked behind the Honda Civic, cut my lights off, and headed to the door. I remembered I left my keys in the car, I knocked a couple times. No one answered. I did not want to walk all the way back to the car, so I decided to just peek in the front window to see if any one was in the living room.

I trusted her and all, but out of curiosity I went around to the side bedroom window. My heart started dancing in my stomach. She was having oral sex with some ugly dude. The first thing I thought of was to run to my car and get my gun and kill both of them.

What really messed me up was she was bold enough to leave the blinds open. Man! I had to do some quick thinking. I swear my mind was going crazy. I just jumped in my car and left.

Later, that night, she was blowing my phone up, but I never talked to her again.

After taking care of a little business early that morning and thinking things over long and hard, I decided the military was my only way out of this place.

The Daily Advancer

Wednesday, March24, 1994
Elizabeth City, North Carolina

**Elizabeth City State University Student Found
Dead
Body in dumpster behind the Dollar Buck Store**

***

Donnie started to read the letter from David. He was talking about how well Maurice was doing in college and how he was helping him pay his way. He was still out there doing the same old thing. Donnie knew it was only a matter of time before David ended up in somebody's prison.

No matter how many times Donnie tried preaching to him, David always claimed to be smarter than the system. As Donnie read on, David talked about their mother's funeral and how hardly anyone attended. After Donnie read the letter, he balled it up and threw it away. For some reason Donnie didn't like to keep anything for more than a few days.

Donnie sat in the corner of his room, his hands over his face. He was glad to get mail, but for some reason hearing from home always made him think too hard.

"Hey! DR 12-32 are you ok?" the CO asked Donnie.

Donnie never talked with anyone but Officer Miles, so he said nothing, just threw up his hand and waved him on, as if to say, mind your own business.

Donnie placed his journal under his bed and lay on his back intertwining his fingers and placing them behind his head. He looked to his right and stared at the notches on his wall. He started to count the deadlines, estimating how much time he had left, wondering if he had enough time to finish his book.

He went back under his mattress and pulled a half inch long metal piece he had broken off a ball point pen. Listening to make sure no guard was coming down the hallway, he began to scratch out another three marks on the wall for the months that had passed.

CHAPTER 4
Officers ... Fall In

Donnie noticed Officer Miles hadn't worked on his beat in a while. When one of the other officers on duty came by his cell, Donnie asked if Officer Miles had quit or something. The officer didn't say anything. He just kept walking.

After a few minutes, Donnie heard Officer Miles voice coming down the hallways. It was like a long-lost friend had come back from the dead.

"Hey, man! Where have you been? You forced me into talking to one of the other guards asking about you," Donnie asked with a touch of scorn in his voice.

"None of your business, sir," Officer Miles said, blushing a little.

"Man! Did you go get yourself ... hitched?"

"Yeah, I tied the knot, the internal bond of anguish, terminated my single status, burned my player's card, and any other thing you can think of. I think I was ready to settle down and start a family. This prison can really make a man think. I just got tired of getting off work and not having someone to come home to. Hey! That poem you wrote me a couple of months ago came in handy. I read it to my wife at our funeral – I mean wedding."

"I feel you," Donnie said. "I know if I was working here, I would sure have me a wife." Donnie paused and then said, "Do you think God will forgive me for my sins?"

"Why do you ask me, sir?"

"I don't know. Maybe I'm getting a little religious being that I'm coming closer to my Maker. The only thing that bothers me sometime is ... that one question ...Where do I come from? How can a man be born with a deck placed in his hands like the one I was dealt? Listen to this," Donnie said.

Life After My Death

I question my mortality
My life after ... my death
A few puffs of smoke
To clog my path
And shorten my every breath

Feeling like my distant past
Wasn't always what it seemed
My life, my death
My living for self
My nightmare after my dream

Coughing up reality
Spitting out hopes and fears
Smiling while I'm crying
Yet I keep on trying
Been sad so many years

Struggling with my future

Lost in the darkness

Constantly pulled to the other side

Walking backwards to my destination
Wanting to run and hide

I close my eyes to brighten my path
And watch as they come for me
Place behind me…
The angels of mercy
Someone must watch over thee

I tried to shake those devils off my back
But they manage to reach the top

The angels of mercy soon flew away

Please stay and make them stop

Now I'm closer to the answer
My life after death has come
Now I no longer question my mortality
I only question where I'm from

Officer Miles stood speechless. When Donnie finished reading the poem, Donnie sat in silence. The other inmates on the hall were all quiet as well.

After the brief moment of silence, Officer Miles said, "The next time you decide to read a poem like that, let me know so I can have the handkerchief with me. Man! When I know inmates like you who have talents like that, I just wonder how y'all let it go to waste."

"Well, said Donnie, "if I had that answer, I would be the million-dollar man."

DR 10-25, Donnie's closest friend on death row, called loudly,

"Well, Donnie, where the hell ARE you from? You better find out soon 'cause your ass going away from here."

"Not before you," said Donnie, faking a laugh.

"I'll tell you what," said DR 10-25, "I want you to write me a nice one before I go, and when they lay me down to sleep, I will have it memorized, and I'll recite it for all those sad asses in there watching me die. Can you do that for me, Cool Breeze?"

"Yeah! Jerry, my ol' pal. Anything I can do to help send you away from here." They both began to laugh.

"Officer Miles, you are wanted in the office. Lt. Barnes wants to see you," said Officer Seymour.

As they walked downstairs to the office, Miles asked Officer Seymour what Lt. Barnes wanted.

"I don't know. He just asked all uniformed officers to fall in."

Once all the CO's formed up outside the office, Lt. Barnes informed the officers that death row was having a shakedown and that all officers were needed. Officer Miles knew that as soon as they stepped into Donnie's room, they were going to take all the writing material they found. Death row inmates were not allowed to have but a few papers in their rooms because they could make weapons or figure out some way to make fires.

When the officers started to search the other inmates, all kinds of things were found, but not in Donnie's cell. All he had was his writing materials in a folder neatly stacked on his shelf. Lt. Barnes was usually stringent when it came to following the rules, but since he had heard so much about Donnie's poetry and good behavior over the years, the lieutenant just acted as if he did not even notice them. Lt. Barnes walked out the door.

"Thank you, sir," Donnie said in an unsure but grateful tone.

Lt. Barnes pretended not to hear him and kept walking.

***

Platoon, Attention!

I found myself sitting on a train with this other dude as we were leaving from the MAPS station in Richmond, VA, headed to Fort Jackson South Carolina, Reception Station. I had just joined the United States Army and had no idea what I was doing. All I knew was that I was getting away from home.

I didn't know anyone in my family who had joined the army and knew little about it. I had the sickest feeling in my stomach. I hadn't been gone but two days, yet I felt like I had been gone for years. I guess you could say I was on the run because I knew I was going to end up in some kind of trouble if I stayed in Camden. I was slowly running out of money, and I was getting tired of school. I just wanted to leave my past behind and make something out of myself.

When we got to the train station, we could see the buses lined up for us. They rushed us off that train like cattle from the back of a truck. This one kid sitting next to me kept saying, "They can kill us, but they can't eat us." I didn't understand what that meant, but I would soon find out.

I couldn't sleep a wink on the train, and that was too bad because I sure didn't get any sleep that morning. We went from class to class, being briefed on the rules and regulations of the army, only to hear them a hundred more times throughout the time I spent there.

One particular class really made me wish I had done a little more research before joining. I found out that my job title was 11-Bravo infantryman/rifleman.

At first, I didn't know what that meant because I thought everyone in the army had the same job. I soon discovered that I had the worst MOS in the army. About forty girls were in the room, and I knew I was in trouble when all the 11-Bravos were told to sit on the opposite side. Not one lady was sitting with us. The guy sitting next to me on the train whispered to me again.

"We will be the first to enter combat – and the first to die."

It seemed like he was proud to know he was going to die in the army. I just went in for the money and to pay for my college. Dying was the last thing on my mind. "I did not volunteer to die in here," I thought to myself.

As much as I like to eat, I could not eat a bite. I had to get used to sitting at a table with others. When I was home, I took my plate and went into the living room and plopped in front of the TV. Unlike the stories I heard and the movies I saw, we were able to sit around and talk. Everything seemed to be going along great with none of the harassment some of the guys and girls on the train talked about.

Everyone talked about their jobs and why they joined. Some joined because their grandfathers were in World War II or Vietnam. Me, I didn't know, really, what to say, so I just listened.

After two days of in-processing, we were all broken down by our MOS's, placed on Greyhound buses, and taken to our duty stations. And that's when the movie "Full Metal Jacket" came to life. Those Drill Sergeants came on those buses, yelling like their drawers were too far up their asses.

We started running off the bus like someone had thrown a bomb down the aisle. The guy sitting next to me on the train from Richmond was so scared when the Drill Sergeants were yelling at him, he wet his pants.

Although, I was a nervous wreck, too, I waited for the Drill Sergeants to finish their routine with him before it was my turn. When they finished with me and started with the other guys, I whispered to my buddy.

"They can kill you, but they can't eat you."

From the look on his face, he was getting eaten alive.

Fort Benning, Georgia – home of the United States Infantry, the Ground Pounder, Foot Soldier, Grunts, Legs, Wildebeest – the place that I felt I was going to die or become the strongest man alive, mentally anyway.

For the next twelve weeks I found myself doing things I never imagined doing. Because of what I had been through in my life, this soon became a walk in the park. One of my Drill Sergeants from North Carolina took a liking to me. He never really said a lot, but every time I turned around, he was yelling at me about one thing or another. Soon I was a team leader, and then a platoon guide. Before I knew it, my first six weeks were up, and the time came for the turning blue ceremony. In order to graduate basic training, we had to pass a lot of basic army tasks. In order to wear the infantry blue colors, we had to pass even more tasks because the infantry was considered the best of the best.

The greatest thing about our pending graduation was that we all were able to go off based on a two-day pass. The night before, whoever had the cleanest area, the neatest wall locker, and the best full gear layout got to leave on their pass that night.

I called Maurice to let him know I was going to be on pass tomorrow, and he wasted no time getting to Georgia. I wanted him to drive my car down so that I could have something to drive once I graduated. He was more than happy to drive because he loved that Mustang.

I was always a neat person and had no problem passing my inspection with flying colors. I was out first thing that morning. The only clothing, I had was my class uniform. I packed a few items of underwear, called a taxi, and was on my way.

"Where are you going, soldier boy?" the driver asked.

"I have no idea," I said. "All I know is that I want to get the hell out of here."

"Then I know the right place for you."

"Where is that?" I asked.

"Victory Drive?"

"No!" I spoke. "Our Drill Sergeant said that we couldn't be down there. Too many people are trying to get over on us and there's too much trouble."

"When was the last time you had a woman, soldier? Six weeks, right?"

"Yes, maybe seven or even eight weeks ... since you ask," I said, thinking to myself that was just a little too long."

"Look, soldier, all you have to do is hang with the other soldiers, and you'll be just fine. They will show you what to do. Here, I'll take you to the Holiday Inn. That's a real safe place to stay."

He dropped me off at the door and charged me an arm and a leg for a ten-minute ride. Right then I knew old Sarge was right because Mr. Cabby targeted me as his first victim of the day. One thing was sure – the Holiday Inn was off the hook. I never saw so many girls walking in and out of rooms in my life. This was even better than college.

60

The first thing I did was call Maurice on his cell to let him know where I was staying. I told him to bring me some civilian clothes. I didn't want to stand out too much. Next on my agenda was to order a cheese steak from Andy's, a little comfort food to make me feel right at home. I sat around and watched TV until Maurice got here. I missed BET and MTV a lot, and my favorite talk show, The Murray Povich Show. *I always wondered who was dumb enough to go on that show and see whose baby's daddy was whose, especially when the girl was on the show four or five times and never found the baby's father. I think someone like that has to be crazy.*

For a minute it was actually fun thinking of something besides my own problems.

Soon I heard a knock at the door.

"Yo! Bro," said Maurice and opened the door.

Maurice walked in looking just like David. He had grown up. He was now in his first year of college and excelling in sports and in the classroom.

"So, what's up for tonight?" Maurice asked, ready to see the town. "By the way, check out what I brought you. You like?"

"Yeah, it's cool. Anything is better than what I have right now." Although I said that, I was really proud of my dress uniform.

After I changed, we headed to the mall. I mostly spent money buying him school clothes and stuff he needed for class. We then went to Hooters to get some of their famous chicken wings and an eye full of T and A, to use the military terminology. He knew at some point I was going to ask about Mama, so he started the conversation.

"Man! Mama is tripping. She is hanging out almost every night. The dude she's with just keeps her all smoked up. I bet you can't even tell who she is right now. As good as she was doing, man, she's back F'ed-up."

"Does she still live in the same house?"

"Yeah, she manages to keep the lights and the mortgage paid. I guess she still has a little bit of sense. I think David sends her money to pay the bills or pays them himself."

"By the way, where is David these days?" I asked because I hadn't seen him in so long.

"He lives in Virginia Beach, last I heard. Heard he was shacking up with some older lady."

"Older lady?" I asked. "How old is she?"

"She's about twenty-eight or twenty-nine."

"Man, that ain't old."

"Well, it's old to me," Maurice said, laughing.

"I guess it would be, being you still wet behind the ears."

"Speaking of wet behind the ears, let's go find some women and dry my ears off," he said.

We headed back to the hotel to take showers and change. When we got back, I saw all of my army buddies. They all had hotel rooms at the Holiday Inn. I'm thinking the same cabbie that took me for a loop also got their money.

As we were leaving out to find the hottest nightclub in town, we met this real cute girl. She asked what we were up to. We told her that we were just looking for something to do. She asked were we in the military. She knew I was in because of the bald head and the smile, but she wasn't so sure about Maurice.

I told her that I just graduated from basic training and that we just wanted to have a little fun. She gave me her number and told me to meet her at her room at ten-thirty that evening, and to bring my friend. I really didn't want to go, but Maurice couldn't wait to get to the room.

"Hey!" Maurice said, like he was in charge of the plans for the night. "Let's just stop by there for a few minutes to see what she's all about. Then we can leave out for the club."

"You got it all figured out," I said, maybe even thinking the same thing all the while.

"When we got to her room, we knocked once, and she was right there to answer.

"Come in, you boys," she said. "What can I do for you guys?"

Maurice wasn't like me, all shy and stuff, so he went straight to the point.

"You can start by coming over here and giving me a little bit."

"A little bit of what?" she asked.

"A little bit of whatever you got good to offer."

"Well! You better show me the money."

She surprised me because I would have never thought she was a prostitute, but she was totally serious.

"How much you are talking?" said Maurice, like he was really serious about buying some. In fact, he was more than just serious. He was happily ready to break her off a little something.

"Donnie, let me see you in the restroom," Maurice said. "Excuse us for a moment. What did you say your name was?"

"My name is 'Alexis,'" she said, using her street name.

"Excuse us, Alexis," Maurice said with the smile of lust stapled on his smirking face. We stepped into the bathroom.

"Man, how much do you have?" Maurice asked.

"Boy! You can't be serious."

"Serious as a heart attack, Donnie," he said.

"How much money? Are you serious? Because I'm only about twenty dollars serious, and I'm not so sure I'm serious about that."

"Look, Bro, you are only out for one and a half days. Do you think you are going to find a woman, fall in love and have sex, all in one night? You are a marked man because you are in the military, and every woman you meet tonight is probably going to want something ... either money or for you to buy her something. Man! They are going to get you one way or the other. You just as well spend a little money and have a little fun."

I guess he had a lot more experience with the ladies. I said OK and went back into the room. When we got back into the room, she didn't have on anything but her smile. And her body was like a goddess. Her tits were sitting straight up at attention. Whether I wanted to have sex with her or not wasn't even a question now. It was only a matter of how much money was I going to spend. Right now, I was willing to spend it all.

"How much do you charge?" I asked. She began to break it down.

"Twenty dollars for head, fifty for both of you at the same time, one hundred for sex, two hundred fifty for both of you at the same time. If you want the 'Anything Goes' special, that will cost you a little extra."

I hadn't been with a girl in a while, so I told Maurice to step back in the office.

"What now?" Maurice said, like he was running out of time. "What is it now? You've changed your mind again?"

"No. As a matter of fact, I just wanted to know could I go first."

"Hell, yeah! Go ahead. I'll wait right here 'cause I know you won't take long," he said, laughing like a clown.

I went back in the room, and she was still sitting in there. Only this time she had that round behind on the bed in the doggy style position. I threw the money on the bed and began to rub on her. For some reason I could not get a hard on. I asked if she would turn around and help me out a little. I could hear Maurice in the bathroom laughing, which didn't help any. As a matter of fact, he only made me laugh, causing me to lose my

*concentration. I quickly regained my composure
and began to tear into her like a mad man.*

*Maurice walked out of the bathroom right
while I was in the middle of it and said he would
catch me later, and that he would be waiting for me
in the hotel, telling me to have fun.*

*She started to tell me to slow down some
and to take it easy, but I couldn't. It was like I
started to take out all of my frustration on her. I
went from having sex with her to beating her ass.
She was trying to get away, but I think I was losing
my mind because I would grab her, pin her down
and do whatever came to mind. As long as she was
hurting, I was fine.*

***

Columbus Daily Herald

*Sunday, April 11, 1996
Columbus, GA*
**China Gibbs, 16, was found dead in a
dumpster behind The Holiday Inn on Victory
Drive.**

**Her body had been stuffed in a garbage
bag.**

***

Donnie wondered why he seemed to get fair
treatment in prison but got treated like a dog in the
real world. He thought to himself, if he was in

Camden, the same lieutenant would have had him locked up just because of his last name.

Officer Miles came back on the hall. He was told that Death Row had some of the neatest cells in Elizabeth City. He was in a little too good of a mood because he went around opening all of the food traps stating he was going to give the inmates a little fresh air. What he forgot was that during the search some of the other guys got some of their things taken away, and they were still pretty mad about it. When Officer Miles got down to DR 35-14 to open his trap, DR 35-14 through feces and urine out the flap. These body substances landed right on Officer Miles' pants and shirt.

The Goon Squad was called down, and everything was placed on lock. All flaps were closed, and the inmate was taken to solitary confinement. Solitary never made much difference because death row inmates were always on segregation status anyway.

Sometimes, when an officer Donnie didn't like came to work on the dead hall, Donnie would complain of stomach problems just so he could go see the nurse. The officer on the hall would go through so much just to prepare the inmate for transport that it just made the inmate's day.

CHAPTER 5
Dearly Departed

Donnie got word that Officer Miles no longer worked on the Death Hall. He got transferred to "In Processing." Officer Miles had been on the dead hall for going on four years and had put in a request to move. It had gotten all over the camp that he had gotten too close to some of the inmates on the hall, especially Donnie. Instead of getting into it with the other guards, he decided to transfer.

Donnie had gotten so used to being around Officer Miles that when he found out that he wasn't working on the death row anymore, Donnie began to fall into a deep depression. He felt like Officer Miles was his only family. He hadn't heard from anyone in his own family in years. He had stayed so busy writing his book and being good friends with the officer that he never thought too hard on the situation. Now that Officer Miles was off the dead hall, Donnie couldn't muster up enough spirit to continue writing anything. He started to refuse help from anyone. He even turned down his one-hour recreational time. He had taken to just sitting – sitting and waiting. It was like Officer Miles had joined the dearly departed.

"Why are you sitting in there like someone stole your puppy, sir?" Donnie heard someone say.

"Hey, Officer Miles. Where have you been, my main man? I thought you forgot all about me."

"I just had to get away from this hall for a while. Plus, some of the buttholes that work on this hall felt like I was being too easy on y'all. Instead of getting into it with them and getting myself in trouble with my peers or whatever, I just requested a transfer.

"But don't you go giving up just yet, buddy," Officer Miles added. "You go ahead and finish that book so I can get rich."

"How did you know that I stopped writing?" Donnie asked.

"They told me that all you do is just sit around and go off the handle about any little thing. Don't put yourself in a position where you can't write that book. You know that book can probably help someone one day. There might be some little guy out there somewhere that can learn something from it. You hear me, don't you?" said Officer Miles sternly.

Donnie sat there with a half-smile on his face, like he was actually writing something that was really going to save the world.

"Hey! Officer Miles. Do you think that I'm going to be famous, being that I wrote a book and all?"

"You might be if you just keep writing and don't let this crazy place get to you."

"I'll keep writing, I promise you that," said Donnie, now lively.

"Hey, sir! Be sure you 'Will' the manuscript to me before you … well, you know … so I can make sure that it gets published."

"I will, my man. I will."

Donnie was so glad Officer Miles stopped by to see him that he couldn't wait to get back into the writing mode.

***

Separated

I have never taken writing classes or anything. I don't know how you would even notice because, after all, this is like non-stop to you – the reader.

Just to inform you, I was getting a little depressed, so I had stopped writing for about five months. I'm back now and ready to continue with "Three Damned Lies."

-- Donnie Johnson

I was at my first duty station: A Company 2/327th Inf., Fort Campbell, Kentucky. In only six months there, I attended Air Assault School, Sniper School, Small Arms Training School, and Nuclear Biological and Chemical School. I excelled in every school I attended, and it wasn't long before the army made good on their investments.

It was two weeks before Christmas. The unit was placed on code green, which meant we were on high alert. If we decided to go off base, we couldn't go more than fifty miles from the duty station. We spent most of our time drinking beer and watching lots of football. We didn't even bother to go off base because most of the guys had either locked their cars in the fence or drove them home until we came back from wherever we were going to be deployed. Nobody knew – exactly – where we were going because so much was going on in the world. All we knew was since we were issued those light green battle fatigues, we had to be headed somewhere in the jungle.

We also spent a lot of time in the mess hall. And that's when the trouble started ... again. Being that we were in an elite battalion, all the noncombatant units gave us a lot of respect, and the female soldiers just loved us, especially the medical battalion. Just so happened their mess hall burned to a crisp and they had to use ours.

One morning I walked into the mess hall.

"Hey, soldier boy," I heard someone say. My friends and I looked around and saw about five female soldiers sitting at a table. All my buddies spoke and even walked over to the table, but not me. I went to the table where I usually sat and pretended not to pay them any mind. One of my sergeants came over.

"Johnson," he said, "one of those female privates keeps looking over here at one of us – and I know it ain't me."

"I know it isn't me, either" I thought to myself.

I did notice the other soldiers weren't getting too far. I wasn't going to embarrass myself by going over there saying anything out of the way. I continued to eat my breakfast, when she, Loretta Smitters, walked to my table and left her phone number. She then looked at me and winked.

"Call me later, soldier boy."

Loretta had a sister in the military just as cute as Loretta was. I wished she had dropped off her number as well. Needless to say, I became an

71

instant celebrity around the company. Even my squad leader tried to be cool with me, probably hoping to get in on some of the action. The word was getting around that we were going to be shipped out in two days. I had to move fast. All of a sudden, I was a pro at getting with the ladies.

I called Loretta up, and she pretended not to remember who I was. I didn't have time for all the games. By now getting a piece of tail was the last thing on my mind. All I could think about was leaving, going somewhere I knew I didn't belong.

A week had passed, and we were still training and hadn't been deployed. I had seen Loretta a few times, but I would act as if I did not want to see her. Sometimes those military girls could get you in all kinds of trouble. Instead of moving toward trouble, I just steered away from her.

The last Friday in each month was called bosses night at the Enlisted Club. All the enlisted soldiers would invite Sergeants and Officers to the Enlisted Club for food and drinks. A way to get to mingle with the brass. After the food was gone, the big brass would leave, and it was time to party.

"Would you like to dance, Private First-Class Johnson?" said someone from behind. As I turned around, I saw Loretta. She looked like she had just stepped out of one of those booty shaking music videos – skimpy outfit and all.

As fast as my head was saying no, my mouth said yes even faster. Being that the first song was a fast song, we danced around each other for a while. Her friends would come up to me and start to dance all close, grinding, humping, and acting all crazy. I could tell that Loretta didn't care too much for that because she would somehow manage to dance her way back over to me. After the song went off, I was headed off the floor. Just then the DJ decided to play an old slow song. Pulling me to her, we began to slow dance, with me being a little cautious at first. As our grooves interlocked, we began to dig in for the long haul.

"What are you going to do after the club?" she whispered in my ear.

"I don't know. Why?"

She suggested that we come back to her barrack for a nightcap. I told her I didn't know because the last time I stopped by, she acted like she didn't know who I was.

Still, my pride didn't stop me from taking her up on her offer because after the club closed and everyone was hanging outside searching for a girl, I was in her car heading back to her barracks. She didn't waste any time. As soon as we got in the room, she went into the bathroom and came out butt naked. I was so nervous all I could do was sit back and enjoy the ride.

Lying beneath the soft breaths she took, in seconds it was over, at least for me. But after I got my composure, I was like Bronco Billy riding a wild bull. For some reason I was always attracted to fast women. By the time she took me back to my barracks, I was hooked like a trailer to a pick-up truck. Whatever Loretta wanted, I gave it to her, and all she seemed to want was sex, which is the one thing I could not get enough of.

One night she came over to my room. My roommate was hardly ever there, so we spent several hours alone talking, watching TV, and having sex like we were in a contest. No females were allowed in our rooms, but hardly ever did anyone say anything, as long as we kept it on the down low.

Monday, Dec. 4, was Loretta's birthday. I asked her what she wanted more than anything on earth.

By then I had fallen for her like a rock into the water.

She turned to me with tears flowing down her cheeks and a slight nose drip, sniffing, wiping her eyes and running her index finger across her nose.

"Donnie," she said softly, "I love you more than I have loved any man I've ever met. If I could have anything in this world, I would have you as my husband."

I sat there stunned. My head was asking me, "Are you crazy?" but my heart was asking, "When?"

"Why are you looking at me like I'm dead?" Loretta asked smiling.

"I don't have any idea where that came from," I said in an excited, yet somber voice. "That is a big step, especially when I've only known you for a short time. How are you going to push something on me like that?"

"So, what are you saying? You don't know if you love me enough to marry me?"

"*That ain't what I'm saying,*" *I said.* "*I'm just saying that we have only known each other for two weeks, and now you are talking about spending the rest of your life with me. Don't you think this is kind of crazy? Kind of ... too fast?*"

"*Life is crazy, and it darn sure goes by too fast. We only have one life, so I want to live it to the fullest and right now you make me feel full. And just think, you don't even have anything in my mouth yet.*"

"*Girl, you are one crazy lady.*"

"*Yo mama crazy.*"

"*Ok, Lips.*"

"*Who?*"

"*Never mind,*" *I said, trying to make light of the whole thing.*

Loretta wasn't in too much of a laughing mood because she went right back to the question at hand.

"*Are you going to marry me, or am I gonna have to give this good stuff to someone who will?*"

"*It's yours,*" *I said,* "*You can do what you want.*"

What she didn't know was, by the time she said that I was about two seconds from knocking her to the floor. Somehow, she must have felt the vibes. She started to stroke the back of my head and rub on my inner thighs.

"*Donnie,*" *she said softly,* "*right now, I'll just cherish the time we have together, and if you just give me ... you ... tonight, that will be all I need for my birthday.*"

Why did I always meet these fine, smooth talking, crazy women?

Loretta had talked so sweet that I decided we would go out to dinner for her birthday and maybe see what happen from there. We headed out to the Red Lobster for her birthday dinner. When we got inside the restaurant, she was greeted with a dozen red roses, which I had ordered earlier. I was convinced that not only did she love me, but I loved her, too. I had Pvt. Campbell, my roommate – we called him "Soup" – to come to the restaurant once I gave a buzz on my cell. I had everything planned out perfect ... until they made the announcement over the intercom.

"All 2nd and the 327th infantry Battalion report to their units."

That meant, I had to stop what I was doing and move out. Being that Loretta was also in the military, she understood that the dinner was going to be cut short. On the way back to the barracks, the silence seemed louder than a supersonic jet flying overhead. I had to say something, so I mumbled a little word of assurance.

"Don't even think I'm leaving you for one minute," I told her. "We are just separating for a little while. I'll be back, and when I'm back we can get married. That's if you still want me when I get back," I said with a voice of confidence.

Loretta didn't let my confidence go unnoticed. She quickly let me know she would definitely be here waiting and promised to write me every day to keep my spirits, as well as my other thing, up — if you know what I mean.

76

***

As Donnie sat with his pencil grinding between his teeth, he began to think about all the time he wasted trying to make something out of nothing. When the time comes for him to say his last good-bye, he wondered just who he would like to say goodbye to. His mother was dead. He hadn't heard from Maurice since he graduated from State, and when he last heard from David, David was living in Virginia Beach with an older lady. That was years ago.

When it was time for lights out, Donnie sat with his back against the wall and a pad in his lap and wrote a letter to Rev. Tavone McKnight for him to forward to Maurice. All he wanted to know was where Maurice was, how was he doing, whether he was married or not, and any other thing that he thought was important to him at the moment. At the end of the letter, he wrote a poem off the top of his head that he thought would ensure an answer.

DEPRESSION KILLS

In Silence
I sat
In pitch black
I see
The storms of life

Umbrella me

Rejection fades
My rays of light
I'm that blue bird
Singing
The song of his life

Misery and mystery
Befriend me
Salvaging my straps
Very angrily

THREE KNOCKS ON THE DOOR
DEAFEN MY EAR
TWO WITH SERIOUS ANSWERS
ONE WITH FAKE TEARS

Behind the glass door
I saw through the pain
My storms of life
Withstood the rain
Difficult hurdles
Were met with hope

But when I asked ME….
Did I love ME….
ME answer was…nope

So...
There I sat with death in my eyes
Trusting myself
Believing my lies

Filled with self-hatred
And non-stop tears
Emotionally disturbed
DEPRESSION KILLS

Donnie figured; Maurice would have to understand that he had to face himself every day on death row. Donnie knew how hard it was for Maurice to face his brother while incarcerated, but it would sure be nice to hear from someone in the family.

CHAPTER 6
All Fall Down

Dear Donnie,

Sorry I haven't kept in touch. I have been so busy getting my life in order that I haven't had time to do much of anything. To update you on just what I've been up to: As you know, I received a Bachelor of Science degree with honors in psychology. My undergraduate honors thesis project was in child psychology. I worked in the research Triangle Park as a junior researcher, a Social Science Researcher (I) position, doing research on children and working with a team of other junior researchers and two senior researchers. Dr. Sherick Hues, director of the psychological research team, convinced me I was a natural and could do credible work in this field. Go figure.

However, I was tired of going to school and was running out of money, so I took my first job as a school counselor to "give back" to kids who experienced what we did. After doing that job a while, I figured I needed to make just a little more money. Still, I wanted to stay in the same field, so I pursued a Master of Education degree (commonly referred to as an M.Ed.) with a focus in Educational Psychology and completed the licensure program for School Counseling.

After receiving the M.Ed. and my licensure in School Counseling from North Carolina, I worked in an alternative school in Wake County. Soon after, the state offered to pay for more schooling, if I agreed to work as a counselor for the state for four years. I went back for my master's degree. I guess Dr. Sherick Hues was right because I went on to get my Ph.D. in a School Psychology / School Counseling program. After that, I started my own private counseling practice.

If I've learned one thing from all of this, it was that we had a very F-ed up life. We weren't by ourselves, either. Millions of children are out here today going through just what we did.

Donnie, I want you to keep your head up and remember, no matter what, I will always think of you as a strong and caring brother. If not for you, I would not be in the position I'm in.

If you need anything just let me know.

By the way, since when did you become a great poet? The poem you wrote me was crazy. Depression does kill. The harsh reality of that poem nearly killed me.

Take It Easy.
Love,
Maurice

P.S. Here is a little something I kept that you wrote to me when you were in training school:

Chains Still on Child

Tested by time
An evolution of dreams
Castaways depart…
On silent beams
By daylight…

Shine
By night...
Unseen
No future, yet told
Only death it seems

Deep beneath the halls of pain
Linked together by balls and chain
Tremendous...
Spirit
Nothing to gain
Only sad memories
Of guilt and shame

Called upon
By mercy and grace
The heels of dawn...
Were soon replaced...
By trembling hills...
Devouring old faces

Still...

My secrets rest...
Within these places
Hidden behind my secret smiles
My future...
Untold...

Chains still on Child

Donnie, I think you had it even then. Maybe you
should have been a writer.

Peace out...Maurice

Donnie was happy to hear from Maurice, but he wondered why Maurice did not mention anything about their mother. He figured maybe, much like himself, Maurice just wanted to go about his life without focusing on the past too much and not letting the present bring too much reality to his troubled life. He knew Maurice had all kinds of skeletons in his closest. Donnie saw the field of work Maurice had chosen as one evidence of his attempts to deal with the ghosts that haunted that closet. Another clue was the fact that Maurice had held onto that poem all these years. The fact that he never married nor had any children also showed that maybe he was afraid of having a true relationship. Donnie didn't even want to give any thought that Stacy said David wanted to kill her and that Maurice didn't want her around him anymore.

No matter what, Donnie was glad to hear from someone in the family.

Donnie felt a new sense of urgency to finish his book. He heard one of the guards say that all death row inmates were going to be transferred to Central Prison in Raleigh, and he wanted to make sure that Officer Miles got his work before he left Elizabeth City State Prison. Usually, if inmates heard a rumor, a whole lot of truth lay behind it. For the next four weeks Donnie buckled down and wrote every chance he got.

***

Rock Bottom

Dear Donnie,

  It's been almost six months since we last held hands. Each night before I go to sleep, I pray that you will make your way back to me. I'm hoping that one day we can get out of the Army and live regular lives like a normal family. Maybe even have a few kids. It's like I'm almost running out of words. Sometimes it seems like love is so complex. How can someone feel the way I feel with you being so far away? It's like your heart is embedded in my heart, so deep.

  Before you go to sleep tonight, I want to leave this thought with you since you love poetry.

  I wrote this thinking about the first time that we made love, so here goes, I hope that you enjoy:

SO WRONG

> Lying beneath the short breaths I took
> As you frantically begged for more
> I ...
> Wondered in and of this mixed passion
> Enjoying the warmth of your body
> Yet trembling with the reckless excitement

of ...

KNOWING ...
YOU WERE SO WRONG

YOU SEE ...

I've held you tighter
Even with more passion
Even more times than I can remember ...

In my dreams

But to live this fantasy

This dream comes true

Defines ... My life ... As it's meant to be

Now ... That you're in the flesh
The reality of us together weighs heavily on
my conscious
Indeed ... I must please you
Yet ... self-fulfillment distracts my every
effort

Until you began to ...

Measure each timely stroke
Until you lost time and began to rabbit each
movement
And each pelvic thrust
And each truss was one of jubilation
And each grunt ... meaningful and serious
movement
Until you could no longer control yourself

And in seconds it was over

Less than sixty

You began to explain ...

You didn't know what happened

You couldn't explain ...

This was the first time this has happened to you ... you said

You just wanted me so bad

And then you realized ...

You couldn't explain it

And lying beneath the short breaths you took ...

I frantically whispered ...

Only in your dreams will you ever waste another of my minutes ...

Man!

**KNOWING ...
I WAS SO WRONG**

P.S. This poem brings back some good memories. And I'm waiting to make more ... Mr. Bronco

Love, your future wife

***

After reading the letter I fixed my makeshift bed and lay down. I knew first call would come early. Alpha Company was the most gung-ho unit I had ever been in. All the Battalion Commander had to do was say, "Let's," and they were ready to "go" – even if it meant we all weren't coming back. The 1st Sgt. and the CO loved being the first out on missions. It's like they didn't have a life of their own. Me ... I had a life with Loretta as soon as I got back home. I could not understand why she would care to wait for me, but I was sure glad she did.

I spent the rest of the night thinking of the letter she wrote and what we were going to do when I got back home. After about thirty minutes, I finally faded off into a deep sleep, but seconds later I was awakened by gun shots from the distance. No one had to say anything. I knew we were under attack. Everyone was trying to get their stuff packed as fast as they could so we could move into our fighting positions.

Soon after the mortar rounds started hitting our position, my foxhole buddy was hit by some fragments. Being that I took a combat lifesaving course, I quickly applied all the steps to save him and then dragged him away from the fire.

Six months later the conflict was over, and we were headed home. The seven-hour flight back seemed like twenty-four hours, and all I could do was hope that she was standing there as I got off the plane. As the plane landed, I could see the marching band waiting on the runway. Crowds of people were standing around, waving flags, jumping up and down, as the wheels of the plane scraped the airfield.

When the plane finally rolled to its final stop, we all grabbed our things, almost tripping over each other trying to get off and greet our loved ones. The post commander welcomed us, and everyone started to search the crowd to find family or friends. As I scanned the crowed, Loretta was nowhere to be found. I had written and told her that we were going to be home on this date. I even gave her the time that we would land. Even the TV crews were out there.

When I got back to the barracks, I called her to see what was up. I learned that she was out in the field on a medical training exercise. At first, I thought she was just writing me to help me stay alive while I was on my tour of duty. I wasn't glad she was out on a field training exercise, but it sure helped explain her absence. She only had three days before she got back, and I waited patiently for her return.

The whole time I was in Somalia, I never heard from any of my family. I understood Maurice and David not writing because as guys growing up, they weren't the writing kind, plus Maurice was in school, so I figured he didn't have time. I thought, for sure, Beatrice or Tavone would make sure Mama wrote.

I started to wonder what was up with everyone at home, getting a little home sick even. I *decided to make a few calls to find out what was going on. Rev. McKnight's was the only number I had, so I decided to give him a call.*

"Hello. May I speak to Reverend McKnight?"

"Speaking."

"Hey, man. This is Donnie."

"I know who you are. How in the world are you?" Tavone said with a voice of jubilation that pierced through the phone. "Man, I have been wondering how you've been doing over in those bushes. Your mom told me that you were in Somalia."

"Mama told you that?" I said, surprised.

"Yes. Your mama keeps up with all y'all. She said she called the Red Cross and found out where you were."

"Why didn't she ever write me?"

"I can't answer that for you. Why don't you ask her for yourself?"

"Where is she?" I asked.

Tavone got quiet for a second to compose himself, and then answered with a sound of assurance. "She is in a half-way house." Tavone then quickly let me know she was doing well and was trying to get back on her feet.

"How did she fall off her feet? Never mind," I said. "Just give me the number so I can call."

"I think it's a good thing that you are calling her. Hold on and let me get the number."

As Tavone went to retrieve the number, I patiently waited. After two or three minutes, he came back on the line.

"Here goes. Do you have something to write with?" Tavone asked.

"Yeah! Shoot with it."

After writing the number, I rushed my good-byes and hung up the phone. I sat with the phone in my hand wondering what I was going to say to Mama. I knew that the conversation would be short and bittersweet so we would not rekindle the hatred that I swore upon our relationship.

"Hello. Is Stacy Johnson there?"

"Yes, she is," a voice etched with kindness said on the other end of the phone. "May I ask who is calling?"

"This is her son ... Donnie," I said, maybe a little hesitant to give out that sort of information.

"Yes! Yes, Donnie! You are the one in the army. She talks about you all the time. Hold on. I'll get her."

As I waited for the lady to find Mama, I wondered how to start off the conversation. Before I could come up with the right words, all I could hear was crying and Mama saying I'm sorry and that she loved me so much. Normally, I would have brushed it all off, but she never told us she loved us, so I had to start crying with her. I knew she had to be consoled because it was the only right thing to do. After all, she was my mother.

"Mama, please stop crying. It's ok."

"No, son, it's my turn to cry. Every time I think of what you boys went through; all I want to do is die. I can't believe that y'all turned into such good men. David, poor boy, he must be the strongest man on this earth because he continued to

help his poor mother when I did nothing to stop James Earl from hurting him. And what's so bad about it. I let him run away, never even looking for him. He was such a young boy back then."

I let her continue to vent because for a long time I didn't think she even had a clue to what we had been through. I guess it felt good to hear her apologize for screwing up our lives. Maybe even worse was how she messed up her own life as well.

What she had put herself through was even more devastating than anything she could have done to us. She had to live every day with the ghosts of her shame eating at her soul. She continued to talk, and I continued to listen.

"David never calls me. He comes to town often, knowing full well where I am. If it weren't for Beatrice, I wouldn't even know he was alive. He stops by to see her and won't see his own mama. What do you think about that? I guess nothing because you haven't come by to see me since you've been in that army."

I couldn't get a word in, so I just let her vent. She finally asked me why I wasn't saying anything.

"Mama," I said, "for one, you haven't let me get a word in for the last five minutes. I called you because I wanted to know how you were doing. I do miss you and think of you all the time. As for what happened in the past, let's just let old dogs lie. Your sons are all men now, and we have moved on, even David, maybe, in his own way, but he moved on just the same."

Mama's trembling voice filled with years of pain and self-torture.

"I just wish I could have been a better mother for you, baby. I'm so sorry. Will you ever forgive me?" she asked, her voice choking with sobs.

"Mama, I forgave you years ago. Just forgive yourself and get your life together. You might have some grand-babies on the way, and they will need a babysitter."

Mama got all excited.

"Are you married? Do you have a child on the way? Who is the lucky lady?"

"Well, I'm not married, and I don't have a baby on the way," I answered, "but I do have this girl named Loretta. I'm thinking about marrying her."

"Have you asked her yet?"

"Well, I was going to, but I got deployed before I had a chance to ask her."

"Okay. You are back now, right? Why haven't you asked her yet?" Mama persisted.

I explained to Mama that she was out in the field on a training exercise and that as soon as she got back, I was going to finish what I had planned.

We talked for about thirty minutes or so until I heard someone in the background say they needed to use the phone.

Mama told me to let her know the date so she could make arrangements to come to the wedding. I told her that would be great, and that I would call her as soon as a date was set.

"I love you, son," she said with a voice that carried deep emotion. She was never a mother who would say "I love you," and I was not the son to say it, at least to her anyway.

"I love you, Mama," I said in the same passionate way.

"Donnie, let me get off this phone before I have to slap the shit out this lady behind me. By the way, they caught the guy that killed Thai Simmons. He swore he didn't do it and that he had sex with her and all, but she was alive and well when he left. I don't know, but I'm sure glad you were nowhere around when it happened."

"Me, too," I said. "When Detective Hutton talked to me, I told her Thai had told me about this guy from Virginia that kept harassing her at school."

"Well, just thank God that you got away from around this place. Look! Mama loves you. We'll talk later."

I hung up the phone and thought about how good it was to talk to Mama. The only thing wrong with the conversation was she had opened a whole closet full of skeletons. I started to dance around my sorrows like my body was trying to release the evil spirits of my conscience. I knew in time I would have to face the dark corners of my mind and search for that light in order to move on.

But today was not going to be that day.

"Hey, boy! What are you sitting around here for?" Soup said as he walked in the room. "Let's go out for a bite to eat and maybe to the NCO Club."

Specialist Campbell was always ready for a party. Since I was just coming from back from a tour, tonight was definitely the right time to party.

"Look, Bro. I would love to go with you, but I have to catch up on some things. Plus, Loretta will be coming back from the field tomorrow. Catch my drift?"

"Yeah, I catch your drift. Wimp. Look! When she comes back, you will have all the time in the world to spend with her. Tonight, it's time to let your bald head down and catch a breeze. Aren't you hungry ... because I sure am."?

I thought about it for a few minutes.

"Not really hungry but I guess I could hang at the club for a little while."

"That's my boy. Let me get dressed. I think I want to go to the Red Lobster."

"I don't want to go to the Red Lobster. I'm going to finish my proposal to Loretta there tomorrow," I said.

Soup looked at me and shook his head.

"Man! Why would someone propose at a restaurant? You can't think of something better than that? How about taking her on a cruise or something? Stop being so cheap and spend some of that combat pay."

Despite all the dumb things Spec. Campbell usually came up with, he actually had a good idea, a really good idea at that.

When we got to the restaurant, it was jammed packed. I guess everyone at Fort Campbell was spending combat pay that night.

Soup went to park the car, so I got out to wait for a table. I hadn't been in there more than a minute when the waitress came up to me and told me that my table was ready. I went over to the table, took a seat, and waited for Campbell. I think he must of parked the car in New York or somewhere.

"Excuse me, Miss. Someone left a jacket at this table."

The waitress continued to walk as if she didn't even hear me. Seconds later, two beautiful ladies came up and told me that their friend wanted to know if I could sit over there with her. I quickly said no that I was waiting for someone. The two girls started making cute little frowning faces and teasing me, telling me to please sit with their friend. One even slipped and called me by name. Then I knew Campbell was behind all of this. Out of curiosity I stared hard through the crowd trying to see who they were talking about. After seeing who was waiting, I jumped up, almost turning over the table to get to her.

"Loretta, what are you doing here?" I asked frantically.

"Gotcha!"

She smiled and kissed me, displaying more affection than needed to be seen. I held on, savoring the moment of this sweet bliss. We sat down and it didn't take seconds before I poured on the questions.

"What are you doing back here, woman? Aren't you supposed to be in the field training or something?"

"Well," Loretta said, with her eyes sparkling like diamonds in the sky, "I told my sergeant what I was planning to do, and she said if I could get all of my work done, she didn't see why I couldn't come in a day early. The whole time I was in the field, I worked my tail off so that when the day came, she wouldn't change her mind.

"The day before we were to leave the field, she chose me and two others to come back and set up everything in garrison for the rest of the company. We didn't have too much to do. So! Here I am."

"Ok. So how did Soup, my ol' buddy, get in on everything?"

"See! Campbell likes a girl in my unit, and he had been writing her all kinds of crazy letters. Every letter he wrote he was asking for some, you know. Anyway ... she was crazy about him and let me read every letter. I asked her if she was going to hook up with him when y'all got back. And she asked me, 'Was The Color Purple?' Meaning, yes, she was. I told her ... to tell him ... to fix this up for me. I told her to also tell Soup if you found out about it, he could hang up getting sexed up."

"She must be fine," I said, "because he didn't mention one word of it. He'll be in here after he parks the car."

"Fool," she laughed, "that boy's gone to chase Pvt. Anderson. She's the one who came back with me to set up camp."

"I knew that fool wasn't going to eat here. Something told me he was up to something the whole time."

Even though the place was crowded, Loretta got on her knees in front of everyone in the place and as loud as she could, she asked me to marry her. I was so stunned that I began to cry like a baby. I mean, she really stole my heart. I begged her to please get up. I began to hold onto her with even more passion. I think it was like I had the passion of a thousand men inside of me, and I was going to make sure that she would never experience the pain and hurt that I had placed on my past relationships. I continued to whisper yes in her ear. 'Yes, I will marry you.' I was so ready to make love, we decided to skip the dinner and get a room instead. I knew she was as ready as I was.

As soon as we got to the hotel, we didn't waste time. We started ripping our clothes off like they were on fire. Jawbreakers didn't have nothing on my manhood because Ol' Johnny Boy, as she called him, was ready to perform. I believe I hit that thing every which way but loose, and she was throwing it back like a champion bull rider. I don't know if we were celebrating our engagement or just straight out trying to screw ourselves to death. Whatever the case, I was in love, and it never felt so good.

After the sex we spent the entire night planning our wedding. Who was going to show up? Who was she going to invite and not invite? Loretta went on talking about what color the bride's maids' dresses were going to be and even how they were going to wear their hair. I began to fade off to sleep with her carrying on about the wedding. It felt good to hear a woman's voice as I faded to black, sleeping like I haven't slept in years. This was the first time I felt alive and ... so wanted ... in my life.

When we awoke in the morning, I was still thinking about how much in love I was with her and how she returned each emotion through the sweet loving stare in her eyes. For once in my life, I had someone that needed me as much as I needed her.

****

Donnie set on his bunk breathing slowly. Shutting his eyes, he listens to the rhythmic sounds of each breath taken. For some reason, even with his eyes closed he began to see a blue light coming through the bars of his cells. Donnie shut his eyes even tighter as he continued to concentrate on his breathing. As the light got closer and brighter...he heard something say, "Goodbye my brother, I am so done with this place, I 'll see you in the blue."

Donnie opened his eyes as the blue light faded slowly away. Donnie knew there was a message with the entity, so he whispered, "goodbye my brother!

CHAPTER 7
Final Destination

Donnie was running out of time. The rumors were true about them transferring to Raleigh's new death row wing at Central Prison. The CO's even got pictures of the area and showed them to the inmates, talking about how much nicer the place was and how they would have more movement and space. Donnie sent word to Sgt. Miles that he was almost finished with his novel and that he wanted to make sure it got into his hands.

Donnie had gotten word, through Maurice, that David was found dead somewhere in Norfolk, Va. Donnie didn't shed a tear, thinking that David had died a long time ago and remembering he said his goodbyes to blue light that night in his cell. Donnie remembered telling David many times before that the streets were going to get him one day. First, Stacy. Now, David. Donnie almost felt like his turn would complete the circle of life and death, leaving Maurice to carry on the family name. With his brain swollen from the stress, the only thing Donnie had left to do was finish his last chapter and prepare for his last breath.

The book, he thought, would be the only thing in his life that would actually make him feel like he accomplished something to the fullest. He spent the next few weeks writing and rewriting his story. He taught himself by studying up on what it took to make a story complete. He wanted to make sure whoever decided to pick up his book, **Three**

Damned Lies, would understand that he was a real person. Before the world judged him, the world would feel his pain. He wanted to make sure people knew he was human and that he felt pain, love, sorrow and that he had shed tears … rivers of tears.

Donnie wanted people to understand, The Apple Falling… Not Far from The Tree, concept was not just an old cliché. It's as real as the sun shining in the sky. He would sit for hours thinking about all the abuse he and his brothers went through as children and how it affected his ability to have a normal relationship.

As he got to the last few chapters of his life, all the horrific events that led to his freedom being snatched away began to resurface. Like a huge wave beating against the shores, his mind began to erode the memories of himself as a person, once loved and respected, now left just as a shell with a torn soul.

Reflecting on his childhood was hard enough, but facing the demons was a challenge that would surpass his unwillingness to leave this world so prematurely. Donnie knew the only way he would die with any kind of dignity was to explain in his own words what led to his reckless and demonic ideas of loving someone to death … or to life. His final destination would offer tears of relief for some family members of victims and nightmares … for the guilty.

***

End of the Road

The wedding was beautiful. Everything went off according to plan. Maurice, David, and Mama actually came. Loretta's family was totally opposite of mine. Her mother and father were still together. Her father was a dentist, and her mother was a professor at Mississippi State. I was worried that Mama or my crazy brother, David, would embarrass me, but they acted like they had good sense. I couldn't believe David came, let alone consented to be in the wedding. I was more than happy that he made it here and brought Mama. He still swears he was the best looking one in the wedding. I was glad that Mama and he were getting along. The way she talked about him on the phone, I just knew they were going to be arguing. I think David must have given her a few dollars. Somehow, money causes Mama to have abrupt memory lapses.

After the wedding, it was on to the reception, held at the NCO Club. Everyone got along so well that I knew our marriage was meant to be. I told Loretta to make sure to keep an eye on Mama, making sure she didn't drink anything or find a drug dealer in the crowd and sneak off. The way David was following her around I think he had that under control.

At one point Maurice called me over. He asked if I needed something to drink. I figured he wanted to talk about something. I eased away from my beautiful new bride.

"So, what's on your mind little brother?"

"Donnie," he said, "I'm starting to get a sick feeling in my stomach about some of the things

that went down. I know you said you were going to fix everything, but there is a lot of talk going on in Camden about that girl's murder."

"Baby, why are y'all over here being all non-sociable?" Loretta asked, as Maurice tried to vent his paranoia. "Come on. Let's get our last few dances in before we head out to make a baby."

She squeezed my behind and pulled me away.

"Maurice," I yelled, as I was being pulled away from the conversation, "we'll talk later, hey! You are the smart one remembers," I yelled even louder. "Get a grip."

Maurice smiled and held his cup up as if to salute me as I faded to the dance floor. On the dance floor I began to think of what he was hinting at and wondering whether he was starting to fall apart. I tried to get back to him to finish the conversation, but I couldn't get away from my new bride.

"What were you two talking about that couldn't wait until some other time?" Loretta asked, smiling with those sexy eyes.

"We were just talking about the good old times, and he was thanking me for helping him with school."

"How did you help him with school?"

"It's a long story. Maybe I'll tell it to you some time, but tonight you better think about how many times you're going to break me off."

"Is that all you are thinking about?"

"Pretty much," I said. "What do you have on your mind?"

"Funny you should ask. I was thinking about baking cookies."

"And I'm going to eat them up."

"Yeah, and I'm going to keep baking and baking and baking."

"I get your point, but you better make sure you paid the gas bill because I'm going to have your stove on all night."

"I hear you talking."

We danced, and then met and greeted family and friends as we celebrated. The crowd started to thin out. Some made a few more toasts to our happiness, and we thanked everyone for coming out.

As we headed to the airport, Loretta asked where we were going. She had told me where she wanted to go for our honeymoon, but I kept it all a surprise. I told her to look in the glove compartment. She pulled out an envelope with two airline tickets to the Bahamas. She instantly began to cry.

"Donnie, I just love you so much. You never cease to amaze me. I thought you said that we didn't have enough money to go to the Bahamas. How did you get this arranged without me knowing? You know you can't do anything without me knowing." Loretta paused, took a deep breath and smiled. *"St. Lucia, of all places? Boy! I'm going to end up pregnant messing with you. St. Lucia. How did you figure that's where I wanted to go? Damn, you are too good. I can't wait to see that mahogany four-poster bed. We're gonna tear those posters to the floor."*

"Girl, you are crazy. That's why I fell for you like a fat man off the moon."

"Anyway," she said, "being that the room is on the beach front, we may never leave the bedroom. I might need to pick up a few more items."

"Like?"

"Like lingerie."

"You won't need any lingerie. I'll want to see you in your birthday suit most of the time."

"Trust me," she said, "you will get tired of seeing my naked tail walking around all the time."

"Let me be the judge of that."

She talked on about our little venture as I drove to the airport. I thought to myself, this would be a good time to tell her about what me and Maurice was talking about at the reception. One thing about meeting someone in the military is you never know what baggage they carry with them. I had so much baggage with me that it would take a forklift to take me from my past to my present. I wasn't sure how much baggage she had, but I knew whatever was stored in her closet couldn't compare to mine. If I was going to test her love and trust, it would start with me telling the truth about myself and what I have seen in my life. Maybe she would call it all off and have our wedding annulled. Maybe she'd understand that I'm a victim of someone's twisted desires and never understood what it truly meant to be in love.

"Baby, why are you getting all quiet on me? What's on your mind?" she said, like she knew I was deep in thought.

"I was just thinking of all I've been through to get to this point."

"Like what, baby?" she said.

"I don't know if I'm ready to talk about it right now. You might ask me to turn the car around and take you back to Mississippi."

"Unless you killed my mother and father after the wedding, wild horses couldn't pull me out this car right now."

"Well, your family is doing just fine, but there was a girl that I was dating who was murdered. Some people even think I may have killed her."

"Did you?" she asked, her eyes as big as fifty-cent pieces.

"If I did, do you think I would be sitting here right now talking to you?"

"Well! What happened?"

I told her everything and she didn't budge one bit. All she said was, I must be a strong man and that's what she adores about me. What she didn't know was, I only told her part of the truth. I just couldn't see myself telling her everything about me and watching her have a stroke.

Everything was going just perfect. We arrived at the airport with time to spare.

"They can kill you, but they can't eat you."

I turned around, and there he was laughing and still looking the same. It was my old buddy from the reception station.

"Sessems! What have you been up to, man? It's good to see you," I said.

"Well, I just got back from Somalia."

105

"What?" I said, surprised. "I just got back from there myself. Man, that was some crazy stuff, wasn't it?"

Sessems got quiet for a minute.

"Yeah, I lost a good friend over there."

"I know how that goes. Say, where are you headed?" I asked to break the conversation up.

"I'm taking a flight to visit my mother. She's sick, and I felt that was a good enough excuse for me to go home. What about you? Where are you headed?"

"I'd like for you to meet my new beautiful bride, Loretta Smithers Johnson."

"Nice to meet you, Mrs. Johnson."

"You can call me Loretta. Nice to meet you, as well. I've heard the story about the 'They can kill but can't eat you' theory. I bet you two would have been fun to watch in basic."

"Ma'am, I don't think those days were too funny," said Sessems, busting out with laughter.

"Well, got a plane to catch. Here's my number. Call me sometime."

"I will," I replied, knowing we wouldn't talk unless we bumped heads again.

"He seems to be a pretty good guy," Loretta said.

"He was one of my best friends in basic. He kept me laughing all the time. Drill Sergeants used to eat him up. He talked all the time about anything anywhere at any time."

"Baby, I think it's time for us to board," Loretta muttered with excitement. After boarding the plane and getting comfortable, Loretta fell straight to sleep. She was so tired she forgot to call her parents to let them know we were in the air. I guess she figured they would find out when we got there. I may have dozed a bit myself. I kinda lost track of time.

"Honey! Wake up! Did you see that?" I said suddenly.

"See what?" she replied, still a bit groggy from her nap.

"I could have sworn I saw blue birds riding on the wings of the plane?"

"What? I think what you need to do is get some sleep."

I readily agreed with her because after what I told her; I didn't want her to think I was losing my mind. I sat back and tried my best to relax. With Loretta by my side, I easily drifted off.

After a while I awoke, and I was the only one on the plane. The only things on the plane were the passenger's items. It was like something out of the *Left Behind* book series.

I heard someone talking in the cockpit. I unfastened my seatbelt, which was supposed to have been unfastened already, to go see what was going on. I started to knock on the door to see if someone would answer. No luck. I looked down and saw water rolling down the carpet. I took it upon myself to open the door. When I pulled back the curtains, I saw the figure of a man in a black raincoat and hat. He was shouting, almost busting my eardrums:

"Cripple cries, dancing lies
"The truth shall come to life ...

"*Cripple cries, dancing lies*
"*The truth shall come to light.*"

I screamed and hauled ass back towards my seat, looking for Loretta or anyone I could find.
"*Honey, are you ok?*"
I looked at her, sweat rolling down my face and thinking to myself, where did you come from.
"*Yes, I'm fine,*" I said, still shaking. "*Why? What? Did I do something stupid?*"
"*No, nothing stupid other than calling my name, then closing your eyes as if to go back to sleep. That's when I woke you up. Are you sure everything is, ok?*"
"*Yes, I'm sure. I guess I got cold feet.*"
"*How are you going to have cold feet when we are already married? I think what we talked about in the car is starting to eat at your conscience. When we get back from the Bahamas, you are going to seek professional help, and I promise you that I will have your back a hundred percent.*"
"*Right now, I'm not one hundred percent sure I know how to really talk about anything. Plus, who am I supposed to talk to about this?*"
"*You might want to start with God. It's obvious this is bigger than you. For now, let's just enjoy our time.*"
I don't know if she really understood just how much trouble was really following me. If only I had told her everything. Maybe I should call Maurice, I thought.

Thinking about this was not in my honeymoon plans. I began to stare at my bride and think of all the good things that blanketed me.

The plane landed, and we began to act like little children, hardly waiting for the seatbelt sign to go off before grabbing our stuff and rushing to the luggage area to retrieve more stuff. We headed to Avis to pick up our rental car. I had tried to have everything planned to a tee.

We arrived at the Sandals Halcyon, St. Lucia. The place looked like something that fell out of a rainbow, transforming us into instant honeymooners. Sheer enchantment danced in Loretta's eyes. She sat quietly as I drove on back roads, headed to our hotel.

"Donnie, what are we going to do first? I know I've got to go swimming in that clear blue freshwater swimming pool. Then I want to go snorkeling."

"Hey! Hey! Slow your roll. Can we at least get to the hotel first, and get unpacked?" I said, proud that I had everything set up so perfect.

"Are you sure we are going the right way. I don't see any signs," said Loretta, laughing.

"No, I'm not sure, but this is the only road on the map headed that way."

"I guess we are on the right track," Loretta said as she started to stroke my neck softly. This trip was more like something out of a movie, except we were the stars of the show.

As soon as we got to the hotel, we didn't take time unpacking. It started with me picking her up and walking with her in my arms across threshold. *After finally getting ourselves together, I reminded her that we had reservations at Mario's for a little Italian cuisine. She put on the sexiest evening gown I've ever seen in my life.*

When we got to the restaurant, I didn't know if I wanted to go in there to eat or just stand outside by the ocean and stare at my sweetie. As we walked into Mario's, I could see other couples looking at us before we melted into the scene, waltzing towards our table. I pulled the chair out for Loretta and moved to my spot to take a seat. With the candlelight burning and the amorous sweetness of vintage wine kissing the evening air, the magic of the night arrived as a mirage of gentle creeks flowed – flowing through my heart, letting me know that love really does conquer all.

We wasted not one day on anything other than each other. Everything from holding hands walking along the beach, to just lying-in bed talking about our future together. We both agreed that as soon as her term was up, she was going to get out of the military, with me to follow. Times like this should last forever. On our last night, we spent most of the time checking out the culture and mingling with the town's people. Soon it was time to head back. We packed, checked out, and drove to the airport.

On the way back from our extravagant, five-day honeymoon, we were totally exhausted. Once we landed at the airport, it was a two-hour drive back to Fort Campbell.

"Are you going to be alright driving back?" *Loretta asked.*

"Yeah, I think I'm going to be ok. Now that the honeymoon is over, can I tell you something without you getting all freaked out?"

"What?"

"On the plane, I thought I was awake ... I must have been asleep ... I could have sworn I was the only one on the plane. I looked for you and you were nowhere in sight. I kept calling your name and everything."

I went on to explain everything that happened and how I was hearing voices in the cockpit and how it was chanting, "Cripple cries, dancing lies, the truth shall come to light."

I didn't tell her about the man I saw in the raincoat, or the water drenched on the carpet because I didn't want her to think I was seeing things as well.

"What do you think that meant?" she asked with obvious concern.

Like before, I only told her what I wanted her to know, which was partly the truth and mostly lies. The problem with the lying was I hated lying to her. I felt like I shouldn't keep her in the dark about anything. I just wasn't sure she was ready for the whole truth ... yet. Loretta had a sharp memory, and she started to ask questions that would eventually lead up to me having to explain some things in a little more detail.

"Why wasn't Beatrice Harold or Reverend Tavone McKnight at the wedding? Didn't I send them invitations to the wedding, or did I forget to mail them?" she asked. She then answered her own question, "Yes, I sent them off because they were in the pail with all the invitations for the North Carolina folks."

"I don't know why they didn't come. When we get back, I call them and find out," I said.

"They could have at least called you to let you know that they couldn't make it or something."

"I know. Maybe they were busy. With him preaching and all, and Beatrice busy helping out everyone, it probably slipped their minds." But how could it slip their minds.

My real thoughts were that Beany, Beatrice's daughter, had told them something that caused them to not come to the wedding. Maybe Beany saw Thai, and Thai told her who killed her.

I remember Beany as a little girl. She was always off to herself. No one bothered her. She just hung under Beatrice. I surely hoped she had nothing to do with them not coming to the wedding.

I started to wonder what was really going on in Loretta's mind. I was thinking that maybe she was having second thoughts about me. I wondered if she felt I was telling her the whole truth. I looked over to talk with her in more detail about my theories, that's all they were, but she was sleeping like a baby. I guess she had no reason to doubt anything I told her because I gave her no reason to think I was lying about anything.

As I stopped at the Main Post Gate to show my I.D. badge, she was still sleep. I had to wake her up when we pulled up to the barracks for her to sign-in off leave. Being that my barracks was right across from hers, I left to go over and sign myself in.

As soon as I drove up to the parking lot, Spec. Campbell and a few other guys came up to the car and started to tell me that an investigator had been coming around asking questions about me. Soup said, like a down-to-earth homeboy, "I didn't tell him jack. I told him if he didn't get out of my face, I was going to kick his ass." He wasn't joking because after being called out on different tours of duty, we didn't care too much about anything.

I listened as they each told me what they had been asked. The investigator was from Virginia and that guy who is locked up for Thai's murder must have hired them. I knew I had to call Maurice and call him ASAP. I went back to pick up Loretta from her barracks and headed back to our apartment off base. As we unpacked, the phone rang. Loretta was in the restroom, and I didn't really want to answer it at the time because so much was on my mind.

"Honey, are you going to get the phone? It might be something important."

"Yeah, I got it," I yelled back. "Hello."

"Is this Mr. Johnson?"

"Yeah, this is him. Can I help you?"

"Yes, I like to know if we could meet somewhere and talk."

"Who is this? Talk about what?" I asked.

"I'm sorry. My name is Teddy Warden. I'm a private investigator. I just have a few questions to ask you."

"Well, unless you have a court order or an act of Congress to back you up, I ain't answering any questions about anything. I'm afraid you just

*wasted a trip. Thank you for calling. Sorry you
wasted your time."*

*As the investigator continued to talk, I hung
up the phone and began to think of answers for the
questions that was soon to follow the phone call.*

"Who was that Donnie?"

"Nobody, just some bill collector."

"Did you pay Rental Center?"

"No. I'll pay them tomorrow."

"Was that who was on the phone?"

"Yes," I lied. "That's who it was."

*"Make sure you pay that bill because you
know I can't be going without my TV. I'm having
them pick all this stuff up next Friday and we are
going to Sam's Club and get one of those big
screens with the built-in DVD/CD player. You know
it would fit beautifully in the living room.*

*"Yeah. Great! Whatever you say, baby. Hey,
look I've got to get back to the barracks to find out
what I have to have for training tomorrow."*

*Loretta waved me off, letting me know she
would probably be in bed by the time I got back.*

*On the way to the barracks, I was thinking
about what that investigator wanted. In a way, I
kinda knew, but I just wasn't ready to face any of
that stuff. Plus, I figured if he had any facts to go
with any of the questions, he had to ask me, he
would have gone through the right chain of
command to get to me. When I got to the barracks, I
went in the dayroom to use the phone to call
Maurice and see what he was trying to tell me at the
wedding reception.*

"Hello, may I speak to..."

114

"Shut up. It's me, dummy," Maurice said like he was glad that I called. "What's up, man?"

"Nothing much other than this guy named Teddy Warden called me and asked could he come over to my house and talk to me."

"What did you tell him?"

"I told him hell no. Well, maybe not in those words."

"What did he say?"

"I don't know. I didn't give him time to respond. Have you heard anything?" I asked, hoping that Maurice was going to finish what he was trying to tell me at the reception.

"I was trying to tell you ... that guy who was accused of killing Thai, his family hired a private detective and word was they found some new leads to justify his story. Man, things are getting kind of scary, and I don't know what I'm going to do if they come around to ask me questions."

"You aren't going to do nothing. Just keep your peace and I'm sure they'll come up empty," I explained, hoping and praying that I was right.

"I sure hope you know what you are talking about, man," Maurice said with a brief pause of relief. "By the way, Mama is back on the downside of things again. I guess drugs are hard to shake off. It won't be long before they find her lying in the gutter somewhere with her head beat in."

"Just keep an eye on her," I said.

When I got back home, just like I suspected, Loretta was in the bed asleep. At least, I thought she was. I crept through the house trying not to wake her up. Being the bathroom was connected to the

115

bedroom, as I came out of the shower, she spoke to me with a sleepy goggled sound.

"Are you coming to bed?"

"Yeah! I guess I'll call it a night," I answered.

I slid under the covers, and she backed that thing up and started moving her pillow-soft tush against my limp, tired, wore-out body. My mind was telling me yes, but my body was telling me to get to sleep. For once, my body was in charge.

As she began to caress me, I fell deeper into my subconscious bliss, fading into my dreamland. Unfortunately for me, dreamland was the place where I revisited my demons.

I was walking towards the infamous light that people see when they are on their way to glory. I, too, saw the light, but this light was reflecting spores of pain that scarred even the breath I breathe. The pressure was building up in me, and I couldn't understand why God allowed me to live this long. Why did He allow others to have such blessed lives and my life was so unblessed? I just couldn't understand. I know I wasn't one to be questioning God, but sometimes I felt like I was owed some type of explanation for the suffering I'd been through. I don't believe that man was meant to live his life to the point that it's not worth living. While on my journey, I had always thrived on living, with love being the most important guide.

Now I'm on a journey to redeem my self-worth and basic being. I didn't feel like I was walking this path on my own. I knew there had to be *some kind of divine intervention helping me make it this far.*

I started to have even deeper visions of me receiving forgiveness from all those I harmed along my way. I remember an angel taking me by the hands and telling me that Jesus walks with all as long as they give all unto Him. All included my suffering and my sin. With the utmost solemn and calmness in my body, I released myself to all those visions that held me captive and asked God to save me.

As beautiful as the dream was, I woke up thinking I had to do something about the situation I put myself in. I decided I would give Loretta a week to get over our little engagement and I was going to seriously think about telling her the whole truth and nothing but the truth

kind of divine intervention helping me make it this far.

I started to have even deeper visions of me receiving forgiveness from all those I harmed along my way. I remember an angel taking me by the hands and telling me that Jesus walks with all as long as they give all unto Him. All included my suffering and my sin. With the utmost solemn and calmness in my body, I released myself to all those visions that held me captive and asked God to save me.

As beautiful as the dream was, I woke up thinking I had to do something about the situation I put myself in. I decided I would give Loretta a week to get over our little engagement and I was going to seriously think about telling her the whole truth and nothing but the truth.

***

The ceiling became a Big Screen TV for Donnie and he would stare up at it as all expects of his life flash upon it until sleep was enforce to impede his thoughts, but   even than his thoughts would turn into dreams or nightmares.

Chapter 8

Trying Times

Donnie was on his last leg as lawyers tried to have his life spared. Experts tried to blame his childhood as the major force behind his role in the murders. They even went so far as to say his I.Q. was that of a ten-year-old, but his records showed his I.Q. was way above 69, the top score of the level that defines mild retardation. Prosecutors argued that Donnie's I.Q. was much higher. As evidence they showed his grades from Shaw University, as well as the scores he made on his ASVAB test to get into the military. Testimony also showed that Donnie displayed no mental problems and was a model inmate while in prison. His final chance to avoid execution evaporated when the governor denied a petition to commute Donnie's death sentence to life in prison.

A year earlier the court of appeals and the U.S. Supreme Court rejected a late round of petitions from Donnie. Donnie knew that whatever was going to happen to him was not going to change the fact three women were dead, one whom he loved deeply. He had spent seven years of his life behind bars and was more than prepared to leave, one way or another.

***

I Tried

A year had past, and our marriage was as strong as it could be. Although I wanted to confess all my sins to Loretta, I could not take a chance on losing her. I went on with my life, hoping all would be well. We celebrated our first anniversary by spending the whole day together, cherishing the time we had had. It had been a year since our unit had been called out, and we knew that it was just a matter of time before we would end up separated.

I only had seven months left in the military, and Loretta's time was even shorter. Loretta was just as beautiful as she was the day we first met. Each time I looked in her eyes, I found everything that was right with my life and this crazy world.

The next morning at company formation, I was standing erect but was asleep. The 1ˢᵗ Sgt. called the company to attention, and I jumped like someone had just thrown a grenade. Everyone in my platoon started to laugh.

"What was so funny?" the first sergeant asked. "Why don't 1st platoon just get down and push twenty-five," he yelled at the top of his lungs.

"Yes, sir!" said the platoon sergeant.

We dropped and started to count off our push-up in sync. As Soup pushed beside me, he whispered, "Man! Whatever is eating you, you need to snap out of it. You are starting to trip. You know that people are around here talking about that private investigator and the crazy questions he has been asking." The platoon sergeant saw us talking.

"Since you two have so much to talk about, why don't you just stay down there and do an extra thirty," he growled.

We did our extra push-ups, requested permission to recover, and stood up in silence.

The 1st Sgt. turned the formation over to the Company Commander. He, in turn, called me to front and center. Then he began to call off orders for a Medal of Honor for saving a fellow soldier while in Somalia. After he pinned the medal on me, the company began to clap and cheer. I returned to my platoon and stood there, both proud and ashamed. A soldier never wins a Medal of Honor. It is a recognition that brings a pride borne of sorrow. Almost without exception, this type of recognition comes because a lot of guys died or were wounded badly. The Company Commander released me from duty for the day.

When I returned home, I found Loretta sitting on the couch crying.

"What's wrong, honey?" I asked. I sensed whatever was making her cry had to be something big.

"I think you better sit down for this one," she said.

"You sound like someone off the soap operas. Just tell me what's the problem. What are you doing home anyway? Didn't you have to go the work this morning?"

"Yes, but I got sick, so they told to go home and get some rest," she said as she smiled and cried at the same time.

For a minute I thought that she was cracking up. I told her to either tell me what's going on or I was going to go back to work.

"Ok. Forget it. Go on back to work," she said, teasing me.

"Girl, what the Flizz Zips Goenzs Zon," I replied, speaking in my best ebonics.

"Sit down beside me, and I'll tell you."

I sat beside her and started wiping the tears from her eyes.

"You know that I've been sleeping a lot lately and I've been so tired that my eyelids barely hold themselves up."

"Yeah! Yeah! Go on, go on."

"Well, I'm three weeks pregnant."

"What? And you're crying? What is the crying all about?"

"I'm happy ... but I'm scared."

"Scared of what?"

"Ok. YOU have it then."

"Oooooh ... I see. You are scared to have the baby. I feel you now. Let's go in the bedroom and have a little afternoon delight and talk about it."

For some reason she was starting to look sexier than any other time before. I wanted to make sure everything was going to be fine with her. I stayed home all that evening and talked about our plans and the changes that would have to come with this news. Loretta decided she was going to get out of the army and go home to live closer to her parents until the baby was born. I was going to finish my last tour of duty and get out ... and move to Mississippi with her.

"Did you call your parents to let them know the good news?" I asked.

"No. I wanted you to be the first to know."

I thought to myself ... she has put me first in her life and now, in my own selfish way, I was leading her through a spider-woven heart of deception. Trying to block out the dark shadows, I could see myself pacing through my head and wearing down my brain. As she held me, I lay looking at the ceiling, wondering when it was going to come crashing down.

"Baby, I'm hungry. Will you go to McDonalds and get me a Big Mac, some fries, and a milk shake?" Loretta said, holding her stomach like she was already nine months pregnant. "Our baby is hungry."

"While I'm at it, do you want me to bring you back a cow, so I won't have to make any more trips out tonight?"

"Funny!" she smarted back. "I'm not even going to start accepting the little jokes you think you're going to be slipping in. Every time you think of a good one, you better go outside and say it to yourself. If not, I'm going to cut you off in the bedroom. Then you will have to take care of your own needs."

I got the keys to head out the door. Then I looked back at Loretta and said, "That's it for the jokes ... because I know you ain't joking."

"Now what the Flizz Zipp!" she said, mocking me as she laughed.

As I walked out the door, I heard the phone ring. Even though it had been a while since that guy had been around, I had this deep intuition that his search wasn't over. I wanted to run back in like I forgot something and get the phone, but I knew that wasn't a good idea.

When I got back, Loretta informed me that Maurice had called and wanted me to call him back. I didn't want to talk with him in her presence, so I told her I would get back with him later. I explained that I had to get up early in the morning for a battalion run. I took a shower and got ready for bed. She started eating like she hadn't eaten in weeks. I watched her devour that food, thinking to myself she was going to eat herself into a coma.

The next morning, I was up bright and early. On the way out the door I asked her if she was going to work, and she responded with a sleepy and foggy-like voice.

"No. I'm going to take a leave of absence for this week. I'll probably go back to work first thing Monday morning."

I put on my PT uniform and headed out the door. On the way to work, I called Maurice to see what he wanted.

"Hello."

"Hey! Why are you just now calling me back?" he demanded.

"Man! My wife listens to everything I'm saying when I'm on the phone. Hell! She will even answer questions that I'm asking folks when I'm talking to someone. So, what's on your mind?"

"Just called to let you know that I was letting Mama stay with me and that you needed to call and talk to her sometime."

"You mean to tell me that Mama wanted to stay with you?"

"Well, she doesn't have much of a choice now that she had a stroke."

"A stroke? When did that happen? Why didn't you call me?"

"Fool, I called you yesterday, didn't I? She just had it yesterday. It was a light stroke. One side of her face is kind of twisted, but she can still do for herself. I hired a home health care company to take care of her medical needs until she is fully recovered."

I was sad to hear about Mama and all, but what I was really interested in was if he heard anything from that Teddy Warden man or if anyone else had been questioning him about anything.

Being that he didn't mention it, I figured no one had contacted him.

"Thanks for calling me about Mama. As soon as she's up and running, tell her that I will call her."

"Damn, Donnie," he said, "you sound like you are talking about a car."

"Aw, you know what I'm saying. Just tell her what I said."

"Hey!" Maurice said, like he had something good to tell me. "The next time you call me, try not to call so early in the freaking morning. Even the roosters don't crow this early."

"Sorry about that. Hey look! I got to go. I just got to work. Talk to you later."

As I hung up, I thought of how paranoid I was. Even though I hadn't heard anything from anyone, my conscience was killing me. I ran five miles at the Battalion Run. I don't remember much of anything because all I could think of was my wife being pregnant. Was I going to see my child grow up? Would my wife and I grow old together?

After the run, the Battalion Commander informed the unit that we were all going to Fort Chaffee, Arkansas, to train the Reserves. It wasn't much of a surprise that we were going, so everyone "ho ruh-ed" and the Formation was dismissed for the day. Most of the time, if we were going to be sent on something like that, it was more fun than training.

For the younger soldiers and the one's not married, it was like a vacation. Even for the soldiers that were married, it was like a break from *their spouses. For me, it was always sad when I had to leave Loretta. I rushed home to let her know.*

Being that it was also payday, Loretta wanted to go shopping for some new clothes. She claimed that her clothes were getting too small. Since I was being shipped out, I didn't mind going shopping with her.

"Donnie," Loretta said with the most enthusiasm I'd seen in her for a while, "I went to my Commander and let her know that I was thinking about getting out of the army."

"What did she say?"

"The same old routine of giving me a million reasons why I should stay in. I quickly let her know that I had planned to get out after my tour of duty was over anyway. My pregnancy only speeded up the process."

"When are you planning on getting out?" I asked.

"As soon as they send my paperwork. By the time you get back from Arkansas, I will probably be out."

"Well, when are you planning on going home to Mississippi?"

"When I'm about six months along. That way I can have the house all set for you when you get out and be close to Mama Smithers."

I spent the rest of the evening shopping with Loretta and put up with her asking me:

"How does this look?"

"Does this look right?"

"Does this fit me?"

"Is this me?"

"Do I look fat in this?"

With every question she asked, I made sure to give precise, direct and pinpoint answers. I didn't want to give any incorrect answers that would cause her to have a moody holiday. It was like she was made for me. I almost wanted to go AWOL just to stay with her, but I knew that was out of the question.

After returning home, we ate dinner, and then spent the rest of the evening trying to get as much time in, sexually, as possible. We detailed each other's bodies like we were two classic Fifty-Seven Chevy's at Old Man Jesse's Detail Shop. I tried to let that baby know just who his daddy was.

The next morning, I was up bright and early, headed out to work. When I got there, we all packed our things and headed out to the airfield for departure. When we landed, the reserve unit we were training met us and led us to the barracks where we were going to stay.

After our first day of training, I went back to the barracks, took a shower, and ate dinner. After settling down, I began to write Loretta.

Campbell and some of the other soldiers wanted to go out to the bar for drinks, but I didn't really feel up to it. I told them to go ahead, and I would catch up with them later. I finished my letter and headed to bed. For a few minutes that was some of the best sleep I had had since I'd been married.

Then the dreams, the nightmares, started.

I was laying there on my back with my hands behind my head, fingers intertwined, and all of a sudden green florescent writing began to form on the ceiling. At first, I couldn't figure out what it spelled, but the writing got bigger and bigger. It repeatedly spelled out the words, "IT'S TIME," over and over again.

I lay there, unable to move. All of a sudden something cold touched me on my forehead and began to mark a cross. Tears rolled down my face and I knew that something was telling me that my deceptions and lies were collapsing. I knew I would soon be facing a force beyond my imagination. All I could do now was wait to see how it was going to play out.

A week had passed, and I only had one more left. I soon received my first letter from my wife. It was a thick letter, maybe a hundred pages, it seemed. She talked so much when we were at home that I figured she was just trying to catch me up on everything I was missing at home.

I stood in company formation, but my mind was already running to my room to see what she had been up to since I last saw her. I was hoping that I would find her in good spirits, and maybe even get nasty letter from her.

When the Platoon Sergeant finally released us, I went directly to my room and took a shower to wash off the sweaty day that stuck to my body. Getting all comfortable on my bunk, I open the letter and began to read:

Dearest Donnie,

I hate to write you something like this at a time like this, but I felt there is something you should know.

By the time you get back, I will have packed all my belongings and headed back to Mississippi ... for good.

I don't know what you have going on, but I've been patiently waiting for you to tell me. You only want to tell me bits and pieces, and if I'm going to stay with you and be your wife, I need to know it all.

This man named Teddy Warden called for you one day when you were out getting me something to eat. He told me that he was a private detective and that he had been trying to talk with you. He said you've been avoiding him. He asked me how much about you did I really know. I told him that I could not ... No ... would not talk to him. He insisted that I talk to him, but I stuck to my word. When you left for Arkansas, I told him I would call, but never did. I didn't call because I figured when you were ready to talk, you would tell me what was really happening. But you never did.

As soon as you left, here he comes pulling up in the yard. I didn't know who he was, so I didn't answer the door. He must have stood out in the rain for a half-hour. I just stayed in the bedroom, peeping out the window and watching until he finally left. He looked kind of scary in that hat and long black coat.

I could no longer sit around wondering what was going on, so I decided to do some research and a little investigation of my own. The first thing I did was call Beatrice to see why she didn't come to the wedding. At first, she didn't want to talk. I convinced her by telling her that you were in some type of trouble, and I needed some answers. She wanted to know what kind of trouble you were in, and I told her that I didn't know, but strange things had been happening. I told her how you were not telling me anything.

She got quiet for a minute, but soon she told me I needed to get my things if I could and get out as fast as possible. I asked her why. She asked me was I sitting down. I told her no and she said maybe I needed to. She began to tell me something about a daughter name Beany and how Beany told her that you had something to do with the murder of that girl named Thai and two other ladies. She said she wasn't sure if you did it or just knew something about it. I thought that she was a little crazy and even a bit deranged until she said Beany tried to tell you on the plane. She told me that Beany said that the blue birds sat on the wings of the plane to protect you. She said they follow you wherever you go. Even though I don't really believe in that kind of stuff, I listened on, because it all made so much sense. She went on to tell me that Beany said she told you that 'cripple cries make dancing lies and that the truth will come to light.' Now, tell me you did not say that on the plane. You said that you heard someone chanting that in your dream or whatever you were doing.

Beatrice said that she asked Beany what that meant, and Beany told her that YOU knew *what it meant. Donnie, if I'm not mistaken, this is the same girl you said was standing in front of your bed when you used to stay with them, telling you all that crazy mess. She claimed that's why she didn't go to the wedding. She says that Beany is always right, and, if that was the case, she didn't want to have no part of you in her life anymore.*

I thought to myself maybe that was a little far-fetched. I bought a computer and started to research even deeper into this. I went on-line and I traced everywhere you have been in the last five years. I found in the Columbus Herald newspaper that there was a girl in Columbus, GA, a sixteen-year-old prostitute, named China Gibbs. She was murdered the same way Thai Simmons was murdered. I don't know if you had anything to do with it or not, but you were stationed at Fort Benning at the time of her death. Maybe all of this is one big nightmare, but I'm not taking any chances. I love you and I trust in you, but my mama didn't raise no fools.

Please don't call me just to talk unless you are going to tell me the truth. I pray that you had nothing to do with any of this, and it's all a big mistake. If you say you didn't, I will believe you and we can go on with our lives. If you did, I think you need to turn yourself in.

What pissed me off so much was how I sat and listened to you when we were on our way to the Bahamas. I listened as you told me how you were molested and how you were treated in past relationships. I stood right by your side, and I will continue to stand by your side ... if we can ... clear this thing up.

That man said he would be waiting for you when you get back, and I think you need to give him a call ASAP. Being that you have about six months left in the military, please clear all this up and come home to me. For now, I WILL wait patiently for your return.
Love,
Your wife and unborn child

***

Like watching film sliding through an old movie projector, I sat on the end of my bunk watching my life run out of film. The empty reels kept turning in my head. I tried to picture myself without her and our child. I decided to give the investigator a call as soon as I got back to Fort Campbell.

When I got back to our apartment, it was cleaned out. She took everything but the bed and the appliances that were already in the apartment. On the counter in the kitchen was a piece of paper with Mr. Teddy Warden's number on it. I picked it up and walked into the bedroom and found some pictures on the bed.

Loretta was now six weeks pregnant and more beautiful each day. In one picture she was smiling. Somehow, I saw right through the stillness of the photo. What I saw was tears folded underneath her brushed smile.

I started to look around in the room and that's when I noticed just how empty the room was without her presence. The silence echoed like Cupid was carrying a broken bullhorn, piercing raw tunes through my aching heart, tearing my heart to shreds. I was slipping back into the dark corners of my mind, a place where I didn't want to be. It seemed dark places freed the demons that toured my soul.

The first thing I had to do was tell her what was taking place. I knew I could handle almost anything. The one thing I could not do was allow her to be out of my life as long as I had some control of it. I knew telling her everything meant that I was going to lose her anyway. She was a strong woman, but I didn't think she was that strong.

I was never much of a drinking man, but I had to do something to ease my mind. I went to the store to get me a bag of trouble. When I got back to the apartment, I sat in the middle of the floor and started to drink straight from the bottle. The more I drank, the bolder I became. By ten that night, I was as high as you could get off Jack Daniels without throwing up. I sat around all that day trying to respect her wishes not to call, but Ol' Jack was telling me that now was the perfect time. It kept telling me that she knew I wasn't coming home and to at least call and say something. I picked up the phone and began to dial. The answering machine picked up and I hung up. I continued to call, the answering machine continued to answer, and I continued to hang up. After a while I decided to call

Maurice and tell him what I was going to have to
do.

"What? Man, is you crazy? You can't do
that. Everything is going just fine. I haven't heard
anything from anyone, and that dude is still in
prison. I thought you were the one that said I
needed be strong. Now you are calling me, talking
to me about this? You haven't gone running your
mouth, have you?"

"No. I haven't said anything, I was just
thinking."

"Well, you need to stop thinking. What
happened to you anyway? You sound like you've
been drinking. I know you well enough to know that
you haven't been smoking weed," Maurice asked,
concern edging his voice.

"Yes, I've been drinking," I said, my speech
slurred, "but drinking has nothing to do with it. I
just don't think I can go on living this crazy lie. It's
starting to close in on me. It's like pressure hoses
being sprayed on my chest."

Maurice, like always, knew there was more
to it than what I was telling. He quickly asked,
worried and concerned.

"Where's Loretta?"

I didn't answer, so he asked again.

"Did you hear me, Donnie ... I asked you,
'Where is Loretta?'"

"She's gone," I said, my voice starting to
crack.

"Gone where?"

"She left me."

"What do you mean, she left you? Are you talking about she left you for good?"

"Yes, she left me for good. At least that's what she told me."

I could hear Maurice in the background thinking out loud.

"What have you said? What have you told her, boy? I hope you haven't gone running your mouth and saying things you are going to regret."

Before he had a chance to ask me, I reassured him that I hadn't said anything ... yet.

"Yet ...What do you mean ... yet? You better never tell her if you want to ever see her again?"

"That's the problem. You see, she's been doing a little snooping around of her own. While I was in Arkansas, that investigator, Teddy what's his name, came around harassing her. She answered a phone call meant for me, and he was on the other line. In the letter she wrote to explain her reasons for leaving me, she said that he asked her a bunch of questions. She claimed she didn't tell him anything. But that was because she doesn't really know anything. She went on to tell me that she called Beatrice, and Beatrice told her that Beany said I had something to do with Thai's murder, and that's why she could not come to the wedding. She says that Beatrice didn't want anything to do with me anymore."

"So, what are you going to do?" Maurice asked, as if he already had the answer to the question.

"I don't know. That's why I called you ... to see if you could give me a little advice. And maybe to let you know what I'm thinking about doing."

"I'll tell you what you are going to do. How much longer do you have in the military?"

"About six more months," I answered.

"Well! You should wait until those six months are over before you go running off at the mouth. Maybe she's just testing you. Just finish out you term, and if you and Loretta are meant to be, then you will be with her. I personally think you need this time to yourself to get your life in order."

Kind of like always, Maurice was right. The only problem I had with that was I was going to miss her badly. I didn't know if I could go without seeing or talking to her for that long. She was carrying my child, and I wanted to be with her. I just didn't know if I could trust her enough to tell her what I wanted to say and still have her as a wife. I guess the only logical thing to do was to wait it out and see if things would just die down.

CHAPTER 9

Meet the Real Me

Someone slipped a note under Donnie's cell door, turned, and walked off. Donnie was resting on the bed, staring at the walls. He didn't see the note on the floor or who put it there. It wasn't until he decided that it was time to work on his novel that he saw the note. He walked over, picked it up, and started to read:

You have about two weeks before you will leave for Raleigh's Central Prison. Try to finish that book. I'll be back to get it before you go.

Miles

Donnie knew that he shouldn't keep the note, so he tore it into small pieces and flushed it down the toilet. He had been writing ... off and on ... for almost two years. He didn't want to write ... just to be writing. Donnie wanted the story of his life to show that a real person graced the flesh that would soon be laying in some cold, still, echoing room.

He wanted, in some way, to take the events of his life and sew together the fabrics that would later blanket him like a winter coat protecting a small child. The despicable yawning of selfishness and sickness altered Donnie. In return he became a monster of a mangled society, a man twisted by the loss of family and the one person that made him a survivor.

He wanted the reader to know that once he, too, had a life and knew what love was. He also wanted them to know that … he knew pain and what it felt like to endure so much torment and abuse, mentally and physically.

He often said, "To be tortured by the hatred of so-called loved ones was to be born in death."

And he felt like death, in some ways, was his only way out of this sadness.

Donnie grabbed his pencil and found enough strength to write what ended his marriage to Loretta and why he could never speak her name again. Only her face in a picture taken on their wedding day could bring comfort to his memories of her.

***

I Am Who I Am

It was coming close to completing my last few days in the military. I was having a hard time because my 1st Sgt. felt like I should stay in. He spent a good deal of his time trying to convince me of that. I knew what I had to do because in the last five months, there wasn't a day that passed that I didn't think about Loretta and my child. I wanted to be there with her, but I also had to keep my promise to myself and to Maurice.

I did try to call Loretta a few times, thinking what the hell, and tell her everything, but she would never answer the phone. I never left a message. I guess she felt if I wanted to come clean with her, I would have done it a long time ago.

On Monday, I went to the Out-Processing Center to get my debriefing from the army. They set up all types of classes to prepare you for reentry into civilian life. They also had different companies there trying to recruit you if you specialized in certain skills relating to civilian jobs. The only thing that I qualified for was working in a prison and maybe management.

After weighing my options, I decided to take my chances and see what else was out there or maybe even go back to school to finish getting my degree. Were the stars really the limit?

Finally, the day came for me to get out. I waved Fort Campbell Kentucky good-bye and headed to the airport in Nashville, Tennessee. I called Maurice to find out if I could stay with him.

He was now working at a special unit in the research triangle area in Raleigh and still attending UNC-Chapel Hill. I was proud of him and could tell he was not going to stop until he got his Ph.D. At least one of us was making a mark that would help break the cycle of our Satan-ridden family. To know that he was going to make something of himself was such a big deal to me. I was inspired to get at least a master's degree in something.

He assured me I had a place to stay with him until I could get back on my feet. He told me that he had to send Mama to a mental hospital. She no longer acknowledged the fact that we even existed or ever had a part in our lives. In other words, she had pretty much lost her mind. I guess we both saw it coming. Even so, it still hurt to see her gone so soon without being dead.

I knew that I had to see her. Once I got to Maurice's house and unpacked, I borrowed his car and headed for Elizabeth City. I also had a class reunion to attend that weekend, so it was kind of a bitter-sweet homecoming.

Maurice acted like he didn't want me to go back there and said that I should leave the past in the past. I just had to go home. It had been almost four years since the last time I had been home. I thought maybe it would be my last.

"Donnie, are you sure you can handle going back home and being around all those crazy classmates of yours? You know, they always kept things going when we were in school."

"That was ten years ago. I would like to think that we have all grown up by now. Plus, I wanted to see Mama."

"She ain't gonna recognize you."

"Don't matter. She's still my Mama."

"There was a time when you used to say she wasn't."

"Maurice," I said with disappointment, "damn it, you really can't leave the past behind.

"Shake it off, my friend, and move on ... move on I say."

When he saw how determined I was, Maurice shook his head, as if in an unreal world, and muttered, "Well, go right ahead, my brother, but don't be all Mr. Pitiful when the stuff from the fan blows back in your face."

As I was getting my stuff ready to leave, he was still trying to convince me to stay in Raleigh. Maurice lived snuggled in his two-bedroom suburban condo quarters outside of Raleigh. He never saw most of his neighbors because they were all professionals and stayed busy in their own little boxes.

I hadn't been out of the army five hours, but I already knew I wasn't going to sit around, twiddle my thumbs, and wait for Maurice to show me a good time.

Maurice was into his work and school. He really didn't have spare time to hang out. I was ready to get something going. I didn't want to sit around thinking too hard about my wife and end up in Mississippi.

I got my bags and headed out the door. Maurice asked if I was coming back tonight. I told him that I wasn't planning on it. I would probably get a room at the Colonial Inn. I told him that I would call him as soon as I got back from my high school reunion.

On the way to Elizabeth City, for some reason I felt like I was being followed. It was about 1:30 p.m. Out of my mirrors I could see clearly and as far as I could see there was no one behind me or in front. Yet, there was a presence I could not explain. Everything seemed normal, until it started to get ridiculously hot in the car. The air conditioner was working well when I first started my trip. Now, for some reason, it was blowing out hot air. I started to play with the control panel to see if I could get it working again. No luck. I tried to roll down my windows, but I couldn't. I decided to pull over and get the hell out. I thought for just a moment that maybe the Devil was trying to show me a little of what to expect in the near future.

I signaled to pull the car off the road. Like everything else going wrong, the signal lights refuse to blink. I then started to turn the wheel, trying to pull off the road, and that didn't happen either. My last attempt to bring this thing to an end failed when I press on the brakes and instead of stopping, the car sped up as the brakes went straight to the floor. By now I was sweating like the outside of a pickle jar filled with ice-cold lemonade sitting in the sun.

I was on my way to Deathville and didn't even need a map. I glanced in the rear view and my two side mirrors to see if any other cars were on the road and ... there I was ... on the road ... all by myself.

"Why are you scared? Can't you see the blue birds around? You are going to be safe as long as you trust them. Always trust the blue birds. They cry for the truth. They want to be set free. Please set them free. You can even save one if you chose to ... before it's too late."

"Who are you? What do you want from me? What damn blue birds? I don't see any blue birds. If they want to save me, tell them to cut the air back on and stop this damn car."

Knock, knock, and knock.

"Hey! Are you ok in there, sir?" a Highway Patrolman asked as he banged on the window trying to get my attention.

"Yes," I said as I rolled the window down. "I'm fine. Why do you ask, sir?" I asked him, trying to figure out what had just happened to me.

"Well," the patrolman said, "I rode past here about five minutes ago and thought I saw a young lady sitting in the back seat with what appeared to be birds flying around inside. Once I got to where I could turn around, I came back to see if I needed to call in sick tomorrow and check myself into the crazy house. I could have sworn there was the blue glow coming from your car."

"Well, sir," I said, "you might want to check yourself in when you get off duty because I was just over here getting a little shut eye. I'm all right now, and I guess I'll be heading on in. I just got out of the army, and I'm headed home."

"Where is home for you?" the patrolman asked. He seemed to understand.

"I'm from Camden. I'm headed to my high school reunion."

"Well, you be careful on these roads. Hey! Why is all that water leaking from your back door?"

"I went through the car wash earlier and forgot to roll up the back window."

"Well, you be careful."

"Sure thing," I said as I watched him get back in his car and pull off.

After watching him drive off, I sat there for a few more minutes trying to recoup. I tried to make sense of all this and figured that I was sleepy. I had just pulled over to the side of the road and fell asleep. I thought, maybe I was dreaming like I was on the plane that day. I didn't fall at all for my own line of reasoning, but if I could buy it just a little while, maybe I could stay sane. Even with that, I could not explain the water on the back seat and carpet.

I got to the Colonial Inn in Elizabeth City around 4:30 p.m. and checked into my room. As I started to unpack, I saw a strange marking on the wooden bar where the hangers were placed. I slid some of the hangers over to read the marks, which read: "Thai Luvs Donnie." There were two more names scratched on the bar: "Yukon Luvs Andre."

"This is the room Thai got for those two kids that time," I said to myself.

All of a sudden logic started to take over, and I knew it was time to face the music. First thing tomorrow morning I was going to call Loretta and tell her everything I knew. I hoped the ghosts that were hunting me would find their way home and I, in return, would find peace within.

I soon left for Winslow Homes to see Mama, maybe for the last time, and then headed to my school reunion.

"May I help you, sir," an older lady said at the front desk.

"Yes. I've come to see Stacy Johnson."

"Are you a relative of hers?"

"Yes. She is my mother."

"Let me check the roster. What is your name, sir?"

"Donnie Jackie Johnson."

"Oh! Yes, come right this way. I know she will be glad to see you."

As I walked past the other room, I saw people walking around, talking to themselves, and making loud strange noises.

"Tell them. Tell them what you know, son. Tell them what you know," I heard one man say.

"Excuse me? Do you know me?"

"Don't pay them any mind, Mr. Johnson. They run off at the mouth like that with everybody," the nurse explained.

What I didn't tell her was that he sounded like he knew what he was talking about.

"Wait out here for a moment, son," the nurse said and smiled. "I'll be right back out. I'm just going to let her know she has company."

"Yes, ma'am," I said, giving her a faint smile.

"Ok. You can go in, Mr. Johnson."

"Thank you."

When I walked into her room, she held her arms out as if she wanted to hug me, so in return I walked towards her to embrace her. But the closer I got, she started to drop her arms.

"Are you Donnie?" she asked.

"Yes, Mama. It's me. It's Donnie."

"Well, come on and give me a hug. What are you waiting on?"

I hugged her and was glad to see she was doing ok. She assured me that she was doing just fine. I asked her what she was doing in here if she was doing just fine.

"I think your brother got tired of me and wanted his privacy. He's the one that told those people I was doing drugs and going crazy. I think he was even trying to kill me. He would bring me medication from his job and try to get me to take it. At first, I took the pills, being he was all smart and

such a big deal at the school. I thought he knew what he was doing until I started to feel sick. Soon after, I stopped taking that mess. I think something is wrong with that boy."

"Well, Mama, I'm out of the army now, and I promise as soon as I can get myself straight, I will take you out of this. Maurice had me thinking you were, in fact, crazy and that you didn't know who anybody was."

"Baby, Mama knows all of her babies, even David. What you need to do is find your brother. Have you heard from him lately?"

"No, I haven't heard from him in a long time. I wouldn't know where to start looking," I said in shame.

"I'll tell you where to start. Start by checking around in Norfolk for him." She paused for a moment. "You know that someone bought our old house. I couldn't pay the taxes on it or keep it up, and you were gone, so I didn't have too much control over it."

"Mama don't worry about that old house. It brings back too many bad memories, anyway."

I stayed with Mama until it was time to go to the reunion. It was actually good to talk with her. It seemed like whenever we had a conversation, it would turn out to be so meaningful. I thought we were really ready to move on.

But that was so far from the reality.

When I arrived at Camden High School, the parking lot was full. I think everyone that graduated from school was there. When I walked in, everyone began to look around. Some walked up to me and

146

asked who I was. After I told them, they shook my hand, told me their names, and invited me to the table they were sitting. I greeted everyone at the table and began to fit right in.

"Hey, Donnie! You didn't graduate from here, did you?" some nice-looking lady asked.

"No," I answered. "I got in a little trouble and went to an alternative school. Then I got my diploma from C.O.A."

"You know, I had the biggest crush on you in the seventh grade, and you would never even look my way."

"I was shy, and I couldn't look your way even if I was cock eyed."

"Soooo ... are you married now," I asked. "By the way, what's your name again." I had never even asked for her name the first time.

"My name is Thelma Martinez, and, no, I'm not married ... at least, not married anymore. I had to get out of that. He was a little possessive. What about you? Are you married?"

"Yes."

"Where is she?"

"She's at home in Mississippi."

"I guess that means you are taken."

"I guess you could say that."

"Hey!" Thelma suddenly yelled out. "That's my song! Would you like to dance?"

She grabbed my hand before I had a chance to say yes and pulled me out to the dance floor. Once on the dance floor she began to bump and grind on me. I couldn't resist returning the favor. We danced off about three fast songs until sweat *began to melt the light coat of make-up on her face. As the upbeat song came to an end, the DJ decided to play another of Thelma's favorite songs. I began to leave the dance floor, headed back to my seat, but she grabbed me and pulled me close to her.*

"You're not trying to leave me now, are you? Don't you feel like getting a little freaky on the dance floor? This isn't against your marriage vows, is it?"

"Just as long as I don't enjoy it." I smiled and held on to her.

We danced off a few more songs, and the next thing I knew I was back in my hotel room with her for a nightcap. I really wasn't in the mood for having any company, but I didn't really want to be by myself. Not after experiencing what had happened in the car on the way up.

I could tell she had had one too many drinks and was in the mood to get her brains screwed out. All I wanted to do was figure out how I was going to tell Loretta that my whole life was one big lie after another.

It wasn't long before Thelma asked me did, I feel like helping her out a little. I knew where she was going with that, so I went there with her.

"What do you have in mind?" I asked. already knowing the answer.

We began to engage in a few kisses, and the next thing I knew she was coming out of the restroom with only her bra and panties on. I asked her if I could take a quick shower to freshen up a little. She said in her sexiest-slightly drunken voice, maybe even a little irritating, "I'll be waiting for you, soldier boy."

While in the shower I decided I would go ahead and pleasure the sweet lady, and then send her on her way. By the time I got out of the shower, dried off, and went back into the room, she was on the bed knocked out cold. Since I was there and she had already given me the green light, I at least wanted to see her breasts and maybe take a look at her round, firm butt.

Like a little pervert, I rolled her over, slipped her panties down, rubbed her a few times, and slid them back up. I placed her on her back, lifted her shirt, took a good look at her breasts, and then wondered, why me? I wished she wasn't passed out. I would have torn that up. Instead, I pulled the covers over her and lay on the other bed.

I couldn't sleep at all that night, so I decided to called Loretta. Like always, I knew she wasn't going to answer.

It was about two in the morning. I just wanted to hear her voice on the answering machine. It had been seven months since the last time I spoke with her. I craved for her voice to kiss my crying ears.

"Hello."

I pause for a moment, not believing she had just answered the phone.

"Hello," she said again. "Who is this? Donnie, is this you?"

"Yes, it's me. It is so good to hear your voice."

"I knew that was you calling me and hanging up. I wanted so bad for you to say something or leave a message, anything ... something to let me know that you still loved and missed me," she said, her voice catching.

"I wanted to say something to you so bad, but I was afraid. I just didn't know what to say."

"You could have started by telling me you love me and that you miss me."

"I didn't think you wanted to hear that from me."

"At this point, anything from you would have been fine with me. I've been here, at home, lying to everyone, telling them that I was hearing from you and that you were getting out of the army and coming home soon."

"Why didn't you call me at least one time or write me? I was thinking that you had decided to leave me before we had a chance to straighten this thing out. So, how's my baby? How many weeks are you now?"

"She's fine, and I'm going on twenty-six weeks," she answered. Staying with the subject at hand, she continued to drill me with one question.

"Well! Are you ready to talk to me yet," she asked, still standing the same ground she stood when she left me at Fort Campbell?

"Did you say, 'She'?"

"Yes, I said, 'she.' We are going to have a girl. Now what about you ... are you ready to tell me something?"

"That's why I called you. I was thinking about leaving tomorrow morning to come down

there. I really don't want to talk about it over the phone."

"What time are you leaving?" she asked.

"I'm at a hotel in Elizabeth City right now. I just returned from my high school reunion. I'll probably check out about eight and head out."

"Are you sure you won't be sleepy."

"No, I can't sleep. Even if I stayed up all night."

"Well, I'll let you go. Just call me before you leave."

"I will," I assured her.

I hung up the phone thinking just how I was going to begin to tell her everything. I didn't have enough money to fly on a moment's notice.

I called Maurice and asked him could I use his car. It was late, and I knew he wasn't going to answer the phone anyway.

The phone rang several times. Then the answering machine picked up.

"Maurice, this is Donnie, I just called to let you know that I'm leaving in the morning on my way to see Loretta, just to check on her. I'm going to drive your car. I know that you won't mind. I'll call you when I get there."

I hung up, hoping he wouldn't get the message until I was well on my way.

Loretta had bought a fine home in the suburbs of Clarksdale, Mississippi. It was about a 13-hour drive, which would give me a lot of time to think on my way up. I got off the bed and went to the rest room. While in there, I heard someone say, "You are going to be set free soon." I rushed back in the room thinking that Thelma had awakened, but she was lying there lifeless as she was an hour ago.

I wasn't the kind that got spooked too easy, but I did believe my mental health was starting to fail. I was seeing things and hearing voices. First, there was the plane, which really scared me terribly. Then the car. I remembered all the stories about Beany and the things she told other people. But I figured that stuff only works if you believe in it. The only problem I had with the whole thing was it seems she has been a part of this crazy illusion from the beginning. It started that night she stood at my door when I was at Beatrice's house, telling me about the blue birds. The whole thing seems to have stuck in my head like glue. It's like she has been following me ... knowing everything ... and wanting to help me. I knew all of this was not possible. I wouldn't allow myself to entertain any of the dumb thoughts in my head. It was like my brain was swollen from the stress ... and Beany was like ... too much sugar in my coffee.

I finally fell to sleep at about 2:30, but not before looking over at that nearly butt naked lady in the next bed. Should I awaken her and really finish her off, I remember thinking.

Instead, I did the right thin

CHAPTER 10
Three Lies

In three days, Donnie was to be transferred to Central Prison. He spent two days doing nothing but writing. He tried to make sense of the three lies that was the focus of his coming death. The three lies melted his dreams and cornered his future like a mugger in a dark alley. He would sometimes look at his freckled reflection eroding in the metal mirror embedded into the wall. He would find himself talking for hours ... beating his brain to a pulp ... trying to come up with the answers ... asking himself why ... yet, not allowing the knife of pain to give him a straight cut answer. He knew his book would give reasons. He also knew that it would answer the questions that had to be answered and bring closure to what others thought and believed his death would bring.

Today also marked a significant day in Elizabeth City State Prison's history. Today would be the last day an inmate would be put to death from the confines of these walls. DR 10-25 had his final call with the forces of life before entering the unknown. The night before they placed him on Death Watch, Donnie watched as the guards literally walked Jerry to his final resting place. Over the seven years on Death Row, Donnie managed to get through these nights by understanding, at some point, every one's time was coming to an end.

For Donnie this day was special because Jerry was his closest friend on the Row. He had been living next to Donnie for more than five of the seven years that Donnie had been on death row. As Jerry passed him, Donnie held his head down with his hands gripping the bars of his cell. With mental torture and despair riding heavily on his back, Jerry managed to muster enough strength to look up at Donnie. Jerry began to mumble the words to the poem Donnie had written for him years earlier.

Born to Die

Fourteen carrots
Dingy grins
Dark shadows
As I awake

Lonely walls
Tears that fall
Why must thou forsake

Too many nothings
Filled my heart
Dirty pillow I do hold

Aching smiles
Am I the killer child?
And my grief be this story told

Nasty memories
Faded my hope
Trying to replace the hate

Once I crashed

My dreams burned like cash
Please ... why must thou forsake

Losing reality
Gaining emptiness
Filled with anger
But Why

My chances were slim
Once I really knew Him
'Cause – like Him – I was born to die

As DR 12-25 faded into the shadows of the dim lit hallway, Donnie slowly released the bars on the small glass window, walked over to his bunk, and sobbed loudly. He felt as though it was just his day to cry ... to cry for someone or something. He couldn't gather enough raw spirit to cry for himself. He had spent more time with Jerry than with his own family. Crying was the only honorable thing to do for a brother, he thought. He then remembered what he tried to do for Maurice to prevent family genocide.

***

Donnie's Three Damned Lies

About seven that morning, I was up and out. Thelma was lying there, still asleep. I think she had a sleeping disorder or something. I left her a note and told her I had a real good time and hoped to see her again in ten years. I told the lady at the

*front desk of the Colonial Inn to give her a wakeup
call and to tell Thelma that I paid the bill already.*

*I had only one thing on my mind ... to get to
my wife.*

*I stopped, filled up the car, headed down I-
95 South. The thirteen-hour ride would give me
thirteen hours to figure out just what I was going to
tell her. I began to go over the sequence of events in
my head ...over and over again.*

*I first had to go back to when I was a child
going through all that mess with my stepfather.
Some people can be strong ... go on with lives and
do great things ... and be great people. For me, the
abuse devalued my soul and spit pain right out in
front of my face. I realized that in my mind,
everything that I could have been had been held
back by forces of evil, forces which sucked my
vitality like a leach in the surgery room.*

*I took responsibility for my actions, the way
I had played my hand, but not for the card fate had
dealt me. I knew that I had to tell her about the
murders ... murders that I did not commit. But I had
had just as much to do with those murders as
Maurice did.*

*The first victim, Thai Simmons, I found
screwing that guy when I came back from school, a
really bad day for me. I wanted to go in there and
blow both their heads off, but for the first time in my
life, I chose to do the right thing. Or so I thought.
My mistake came when I told Maurice about what
happened. Instead of him talking me out of it, he
started telling me how I should kill them both. I just
could not see myself going to jail for something like*

that, and it sure wasn't worth dropping out of school.

Maurice was only sixteen at the time, and he thought just like a sixteen-year-old fool would think. After listening to him, I decided to just head back to Raleigh, forget her, and focus totally on school. It was late that evening when I got back to school. I got a call in my dorm room. It was Maurice.

"Donnie," he said, "I took care of it for you."

"Took care of what?" I paused. "Aw. Come on, man! You didn't go and do nothing crazy, did you?"

"Yo, man! I killed her," Maurice said.

I found that although he had killed her, I had to clean up the mess. He left the knife in her back, so I had to go to retrieve it. Second, he always wore my clothes, so I told him to burn everything. So that was the last of that ... I thought.

I'd been covering for him since. Even the night in Fort Benning when I was with that prostitute. He must have had Satan in his blood stream by then. I told him about the rough sex I had with the poor girl, and damned if he didn't go back, find the girl, and kill her, saying that he didn't want her to tell anyone and cause me to get kicked out of the military.

Why did he always come back and tell me about his murders? I did not understand. I guess that was how he released it from his conscience onto mine. All these years, I've been his dirty pillow to sleep at night.

I didn't know what Loretta was going to do or say. All I knew was that I wanted her to know I could not kill anyone. As much as I hated my stepfather, I only wanted him dead after he kept doing those crazy antics. Mama always said that Maurice saw too much growing up and that if one of us was going to get into something, it was going to be him. She said he was like a bomb ready to explode.

I got halfway there. I pulled over to a rest stop and called Loretta to let her know where I was. She answered, sounding all happy and trying to give me the directions to the house. I heard the doorbell ringing in the background.

"Donnie, hurry home," she said. "I have to go. Someone's at the door. Love you."

"I love you, too," I said softly.

After using the rest room and gassing up the car, I jumped in and burned rubber like I was on the drag strip. I thought, maybe Loretta knew I just loved her too much to ever hurt her ... or anybody. I just didn't know if she was willing to hear such a dark secret. My future with her seemed to be glowing brighter and brighter.

Around 11 p.m. I finally pulled into the driveway. The front porch light was on, so I was able to check the number on the house to make sure I had the right one. I was so excited that I hopped out of the car almost before cutting off the engine. I ran to the house, almost tripping and falling flat on my face.

As I knocked on the door, it swung slowly open by itself. The television was playing downstairs and I could hear the shower running upstairs. I figured that she was up there getting ready so that she could look pretty for me. I could not wait for her to come down. I began to tiptoe up the stairs so that she could not hear me come in. When I got to the bedroom door, it was already open. I went inside the room. I called her name, but she did not answer. I walked towards the bathroom. I saw her lying on the floor, face down, blood all over. The phone was placed close by her body like she was trying to call for help. I wasn't sure if the baby was dead or alive. I didn't know how long she had been lying there. I got on the phone, called 9-1-1, and gave directions to where she was. I told them she had been shot. They tried to keep me on the line, but I hung up.

I took a blanket from the bed and placed it over her. I didn't want her to get cold. She had always sat on the couch with a blanket pulled around her whenever we watched TV. I knew she would have wanted to be snug and warm.

I began to go stir crazy. I just wanted to stand there. I couldn't face leaving her, but I had too. I had to fix this before it was too late. My grieving turned into panic, and I thawed my emotions enough to realize leaving her was my only alternative. I shot out the door, guilty as sin ... as far as I was concerned.

I didn't know what to do, so I did what any lost soul would do ... I ran. I ran fast and I ran hard. Although I had nothing to do with her death, I felt like it was me who killed her. The sad part was I knew her death was one more chapter in a twisted story. I didn't even have to wonder who killed my wife and unborn child. I knew.

Maurice had been calling himself saving me, but all the time, he was killing me. Leaving dark trails with deep potholes to the left of me while I desperately searched for that smooth paved road on the right. Now he had destroyed the one person who made my life worth living. The only choice I had was to take his life. I WAS HIS KEEPER, and I wanted to make sure that no one else would ever feel his wrath. I knew he kept a gun under the seat of his car. From the time he wanted to end James Earl's life years ago, guns always made him feel safe. The next time he saw this piece of steel, it would be kissing him good-bye.

To make sure I was on the right track about Maurice killing my wife and child, I called RDU airport to see if any fights had left that morning for Clarksdale, Mississippi. Once that was confirmed, I checked to see if Maurice was on the plane. That was also confirmed. Last, I checked all the car rentals in Clarksdale to see if he rented a car. That, too, was an affirmative. That's why I never got a call from him. As far as I was concerned, he was guilty.

I drove through two states thinking of what I was going to say before I murdered my own flesh and blood. I had so much to cry for that I could no longer shed tears. My weary eyes and abandoned dreams stripped away each moment of hope. I was left only with the demons that helped raised me, the spirits that helped direct my path to destruction.

After I completed this last phase of this path, I knew I had to turn myself in.

I was my brother's keeper. I had promised I would take care of him. By no means could I forgive him for killing Loretta. If I were to turn him in, it would simply mean the state would determine his outcome. I had to be the one to correct what James Earl destroyed. No matter what, I was going to end up doing time. Whether I turned him in or not, I played a big part in the murders, even if I didn't mean to.

The whole time I headed back to North Carolina, I kept looking out the rear-view mirror, wondering when I was going to be pulled by the police. But I made it all way back to North Carolina before I ran into trouble. I didn't even notice I was going 85 miles an hour in a 65 mile an hour zone. Worst, I was sleepy because I had not slept in almost two days. I know I had to have been swerving all over the road.

I was calm as the policeman walked up to the car. I figured if I was going to go down, this was as good of a time as any.

"Sir, could you step out of the car?" the police officer said firmly.

I got out of the car with my heart beating down my legs. It soon found its way up my chest and finally was coming out of my mouth.

"What's the problem, Officer?" I weakly said.

"Are you in a rush?" he said.

"No, not really, sir. Did I do something wrong?"

"Yes, you were going 89 in a 65-mile an hour zone. You also have been crossing the median for the last five miles. Have you been drinking, sir?" he asked me.

"No, I haven't, Officer."

"Would you mind taking a sobriety test for me?"

I knew I hadn't been drinking. A DWI was the last thing I was worried about. I was just hoping that he didn't ask if he could search my car.

I blew into the little tube several times, and the test showed I was more than competent for driving.

After the test, he began to shift gears and asked about my driving fast. I started offering my best excuses, kept smiling in an effort to stay Mr. Friendly. I decided I was not going to argue about a speeding ticket. I just waited for the ticket.

He asked me about this being Maurice's car. I was shocked when he just told me to slow down a little ... keep it at a safe speed ... and allowed me to leave.

With all that had gone bad in my life, I knew this was a set up for worst things to come. I pulled back onto the road, headed toward North Carolina. I figured if I was going to hear subliminal messages on the radio telling me to go back to be with my wife, now would be the time for those messages to start.

Even with the sun at its highest peak, black serenity was the eye of the storm that was brewing in my head. My wife, the one who had kept me alive all these years, was taken away and love was now gone. The one person I promised I would never let anything happen to was the person who killed her ... and he probably didn't think twice about her or me. I knew I had to rush back to find him because the police would soon make the connection between Loretta's murder and me, and then every cop on the road would be looking for me.

I called his cell, but he would not answer. I think he knew I was looking for him. And he knew, or should have known, that I was not going to let him live after what he did to Loretta ... and to me. As I turned onto I-40 East headed to Cary, my last ride to freedom, I was brought to a stop. I think every police officer in Wake County was waiting for me. When I looked in my rear-view mirror, I saw I was being followed by every patrol car in Wake County. I just knew the word was out about the murder of my wife and I knew that I was the prime suspect.

At this point, I was no longer thinking about Maurice and what price he had to pay. I was now shifting back, hoping that he got away. Maurice would now have to live with the monsters in his head. His life was finally out of my hands ... for now. With what I was about to face, I no longer was needed on this earth anyway. I just braced myself for the next chapter of my horrific life.

About ten or twenty cops jumped out of their cars and headed to my vehicle with guns drawn. I got out of the car with my hands behind my head. They began reading my rights and asking me questions. I couldn't do anything but nod as if to say yes, I understand.

When they got me to the police station, I was allowed one phone call. I had no one to call but Maurice. Since this sensational story was being broadcast all over the state, I knew he was somewhere watching me on the news. I had his car, and he knew he would get a call by the police to identify it and be questioned himself.

"I can't talk right now," Maurice said. "What do you want? I got you a lawyer, the best money can buy. He will be there first thing tomorrow morning. Just don't answer anything until he gets there. I'll talk to you soon. Love you, man. Talk to you later."

It was like, somehow, he knew I was not going to place him into this. The way Maurice was talking, he wasn't about to turn himself in and was almost sure I wasn't going to say anything.

I was so confused. I placed my hands over my face and let the warmth of my breath become a toxic antidote to help me keep my thoughts in check. The last time I was in a cell, I was about fifteen or sixteen years old. All my life, even when I called myself getting right, I knew for some reason I would find myself back in the system. I just couldn't believe that it would be by the hands of my own blood.

The next morning my lawyer arrived on time ... just like Maurice said he would. The jailers came to get me out of my holding cell and took me into this small room where he and I could be alone. The first thing he asked me was how did the bloody clothes and knife with my fingerprints get into Mama's old house. I started to think long and hard because I thought that Maurice had taken care of that like I told him. Pretending like I had no clue to what he was talking about, I started to ask questions of my own.

"Why am I here?" I asked.

"You are here for the murder of Thai Simmons."

"Thai Simmons," I said in shock.

"Yes," he replied. "Thai Simmons."

"I thought they caught the guy that did that."

"Well, everybody did until the people that bought your mother's house found those clothes and bloody knife in a bag under the back porch. They matched the blood on the clothes Thai was wearing when they found her. The knife also proved to be the murder weapon. The boy's family hired a private detective, bought the house, and searched it with a fine-tooth comb. It paid off. For them, anyway. Now, if you want me to help you, you are going to have to do some talking."

As he continued to talk, it was like I was tone deaf because I couldn't hear anything he was saying. All I could hear was my heart beating in my ears. All I could think about was how long would it be before they killed me. I knew I wasn't going to tell on Maurice. He had done so much more than any of Mama's other sons, and since I couldn't take his life, I was not letting the state or anybody else be his keeper. I guess dying was my only choice.

My lawyer soon stopped talking and was waved to the door through the little glass. He walked out for about five minutes, came back.

"Son, you are in bigger trouble than I thought." He then began to question me again. "Where were you coming from when you were stopped by the police?"

I was hesitant for a moment, and then realized in this case the truth would only set me free, mentally anyway. I would never be free again physically. So, I told him the truth – even if it was not the whole truth. With sand-like tears, I began to explain what happened and how she was already dead when I got there.

"Why run then?"

I tried to make him understand, but from the look on his face I could tell that he wasn't buying any of it. I knew I was in deep trouble if my own lawyer didn't believe me. I was thinking there was no way any jury in the state of North Carolina or Mississippi was going to believe me.

I sat in jail for a year before I had a trial. While in jail I met a few guys I was in training school with. They all said I was not the killer and that they know who was. I never said anything. I just kept to myself and waited for my day in court.

One thing about those guys in jail, they would get you talking and then, just to get out of the cell for a little break, would go and testify either for you or against. No one gave validity to what they were saying.

On the day of my trial, I was found guilty of first-degree murder in the death of Thai Simmons. My lawyer called himself fighting to keep me alive even though he thought I was guilty. The jurors didn't waste any time in deliberation and found me guilty. The worst part of the trial was sitting and listening to her family as they told the court how they thought I should die for this crime and how someone like me shouldn't stay on this earth. The funny thing was that when Thai was alive, they never even cared much for her.

As far as I was concerned ... I was already dead. I was sentenced to death for my crime – the crime that I accepted because I knew there was no way out, no matter what I could have done.

After sentencing, I was extradited to Mississippi, where I waited another six months for the trial that proved me to be the murderer of my wife and unborn child. You can best believe that Mr. and Mrs. Smithers couldn't wait for me to be sentenced. They hired the best lawyer that money could buy, cursed me, and prayed that I burn in hell.

I was sentenced to two life terms for Loretta and our unborn child. The state spared my life only because they lacked the evidence, they needed to condemn me to death. Maybe it was because I couldn't die but once. Anyway, the jury in Mississippi did not give me the death penalty.

Once the trial was over, I was sent back to North Carolina for my execution. If I somehow came back from the dead, I was to come back to Mississippi and do about two hundred more years.

I understood what love was more than ever before.

I now understood what it meant to live for something and to die for someone.

I had lived and was sentenced to die for accepting what life had promised. Life promised me a chance to experience a home away from home. Life promised that if I tried to live right, only good things would come. There was a lesson in there somewhere, but I guess I must have missed it. My only hope was that I would have shed enough tears to get God's attention. I knew I had to get right with God. I wanted my last days to be filled with sweet nectar dreams of heaven and not the venomous poisons of this fang-bitten earth. There was nothing that could stop me from meeting Him.

I tried not looking at my execution as my ending, but as the beginning of a new life with God ... up in Heaven.

Man had set his date and it was not really the date that God may have wanted me to leave, but now to meet Him was now my only wish. I began to pray each and every day for his mercy and forgiveness.

The life that some of you live, I only dreamed of living. I think from the day I was born I didn't stand a chance ... until now. I've already started to feel a certain peace and calmness within.

When I first got off that prison bus they called the Gray Goose, in front of inmates and officers, I fell to my knees and began to ask God to forgive me for my purpose and my reason for living. I knew that my purpose and reason for living were not His doing. I knew there was an opposite force that we are born into called sin. I prayed that He would forgive me for my sins and forgive those who had sinned in my name. The guards didn't seem to mind as I cried out to the heavens. I found out quickly that finding your religion and reading were the two things you did in here to survive.

***

Donnie had been up for the most part of the night. He tried to sleep, but for some reason he was starting to feel sick. He had been fasting, hoping that all the praying he was doing was being heard. It had been years since he had an encounter with the voices that had always seemed to guide him to righteousness. Tonight, he would have an unexpected guest, and, for some reason, it was time.

His stomach started to turn flips. Donnie decided to get off his bunk and head to the toilet. Once up, something pushed him back on to the bed and pinned him down. Despite the dim light that slipped into the cell, he still could not see anyone. Like all the other times before, he began to hear the soft voice of a little girl:

"Donnie, your cries have been heard and ... your cries have been honored. When the blue birds fly away, they will take you with them. You are setting them free; your writings will set them free. He is his own keeper, and he must face the crows. They will take him away as well."

"Who are you?" Donnie asked. "Why have you been with me all these years?" He paused. "Why do you talk in circles?"

The voice started to fade away but answered. This time, the voice did not respond in riddles.

"I'm that little girl who stood in front of your door. I've loved you forever and watched over you. I wanted to change your destiny, but I couldn't. I could only be your guide. The blue birds will take you home."

As the voice misted into the shaded light, Donnie pulled himself off the bed, ran to his cell door, gripped the bars on the small window, and began to talk with God. With his mouth hung low and face covered with tears, he began to yell out.

"Thank you, God, for hearing my cries. Thank you, Jesus, for saving me."

As Donnie continued to pray, his tears were mixtures of mercy and grace. He knew now that it was time to go home.

The next morning, when Donnie awoke, he was curled by his door.

"DR 12-32 are you all, right?" one of the officers asked.

"Yes, sir, I'm fine. It's just that I couldn't sleep a wink last night."

The officer was surprised a little. Everyone on the unit knew that Donnie never said anything to any of the officers, except Officer Miles. The officer took advantage of Donnie's new willingness to speak.

"What happened to you? Your face seems to have aged twenty years. Since when did you start wearing a beard – especially a beard that long? As a matter of fact, I don't remember you ever having a beard before yesterday."

Donnie just smiled.

"I guess it's time for me to go home and I'm just getting ready." Then he went back over to his bunk.

As the officer left to check on the other two inmates, he slipped a note into Donnie's cell. Donnie rushed to retrieve the paper. It was a note from Officer Miles:

Hey, Buddy! Hope you are finished because you leave in the next few days for Central. Leave the book with the officer that gave you this note before he gets off his shift. He will make sure I get it.

Again, Donnie knew enough to dispose of the note, so he quickly flushed it down the commode. Because he had only twelve hours to finish his work, Donnie started right away on his last chapter, hoping to have all he wanted people to know about him on paper before the officer's shift was over.

***

When I stepped into my cell for the first time, I thought that my life was over. I couldn't eat or sleep; all I could do was cry. It felt something like when I first joined the army.

The one person that I knew would be here for me, because of what I did to save him, wrote me only once or twice and that was to tell me how well he was doing.

I found out about my mother being dead while in here. I also learned about the death of my brother David while I was in this cell. David was out of the frame before the family picture was ever taken. In a way, it was like he was always gone. But the one thing I respected about him was this: he never did anything to hurt anyone but himself, and through it all he loved his family.

Soon after finding out about Mama's death, I spent days wishing I could have helped her more than I did. I wish I could have taken her out of the situation she had placed herself in. I understood that I had no choice in the matter. One thing about being in here for the rest of your life is, you learn to get over all things or you die wishing you could have.

I wanted to help Maurice, but it was too late for him. By me not wanting to let him take care of his own responsibilities, he walked around feeling almost invincible. In time, that will all change for him.

Last night I had a vision and one of the things that appeared was as clear as day. I heard this voice saying Maurice would now pay for his sins. The voice said that my writings would set him free and that he is his own keeper. I knew whoever was speaking to me had to be talking about this book.

I no longer have to take his sins to my grave.

Like most things we try to take control of, we must often remember that all things should be left in God's hand. I have now found peace and comfort in knowing that my life was not lived totally in vain.

I decided to write this book for everyone out there who thought that I should be put to death.

I just wanted to let them know that I tried.

I tried to live with the abundance of inner peace that every man would love to have.

I tried to live the way God intended. I never meant to hurt anyone, mentally or physically.

Some people live and die by the rule that only God can judge them, but I think different. While you are on this earth, man judges you. He judges how you live and how you die. If you're a poor man, society looks down on you like you have failed to live up to the rich man's standards, and it's the rich man that was your judge. I learned to live for myself and hold my head up high, not caring about what people said about me. I tried to let the life I lived speak for me.

Seems like "the lack of" causes us to live a lackluster life, and my life was placed right into the hands of the "have not" from birth. I now live off the fact that I was before I was.

This young preacher once said, it's all about faith and the effort you put forth. The principles work the same for the believers and nonbelievers. God wants all to be prosperous. It's the acting on faith that makes the difference. You can't taste the fruit until you put it in your mouth.

I think I just waited too long to take a bite.

But that's when you use the inner peace to keep you moving in heaven's direction. The poorer you are, the harder you pray and the better chance you have of getting into heaven. With that embedded in my brain, I smile sometimes, thinking of how I must have been born into my situation just to return to heaven. Thank God, I kept the faith.

Tomorrow or soon after, I leave Elizabeth City State Prison after spending seven years here and will head for Raleigh's Central Prison where I will be put to death ... or released to life, depending on how you look at it.

Yes, I am scared. But I'm not scared of dying. I'm simply scared of the unknown. I never liked being alone and, even after eight years of incarceration, I'm still not so sure that I want to lay on that table by myself.

Anybody care to join me?

Anyway.

I hope my story changes your mind a little when it comes to the judgment you pour out on other human beings. We all handle things differently in life.

I am sure there are others in the same boat as I was in yet ended up becoming well known and respected in their fields. Entertainers, lawyers, government officers, medical doctors, maybe even someone with a Ph.D. in School Psychology, like Maurice. Any of them could have been in my shoes. The problem is, we are all made up of different mechanisms and have different survival techniques. How I coped with my situation and how David or Maurice dealt with theirs may have been a lot different than others. It doesn't mean someone who went on to greatness was not affected.

There are a lot of well-known people coming out of the closet these days and some of you may wonder, "Hmmm ... "What happen to them?"

Well! I'll tell you.

They may have been abused as a child. Probably by someone close, like a parent, aunt or uncle, or maybe even a well-respected person in the community like a priest or pastor. Physically, mentally or sexually, abuse is abuse.

And just maybe these victims were afraid to tell. Worried about how they were going to be ... judged.

I told ... and maybe that was part of my healing.

One thing I can say about my ordeal is, it still hurts me to this day. As I head on to bigger and better things, I trust that something I wrote may help someone who has walked that long mile. I also hope the next time you hear some lawyer in court or on TV talking about their client's troubled childhood, you won't brush it off as mere gibberish. I hope you will hear a solemn cry in there somewhere.

Well, if you are reading this in book form, that means Officer Miles did what he said he was going to do. If you see Maurice on TV, that means a few detectives have read the manuscript before it was published.

And if Officer Miles is still working at the prison, that means my book didn't end up on New York Times Bestsellers List.

Sorry.

But I think my work is done and I must go.

Thanks for taking your time to get to know
me.

See you in the after world.

The End

P.S. I added on a book of poetry entitled 'Flight of the Blue Bird.' I hope you will enjoy as well.
Donnie Jackie Johnson

CHAPTER 11
Cripple Cries

After Donnie felt the book was complete, he placed it on the food trap for the officer to pick up before he left his shift. Donnie didn't have time to read over the last chapter, but he felt his message got through.

Just like Officer Miles said, the officer that was on duty came by and picked up the manuscript and kept walking.

Moving inmates from one prison to the next is a sensitive process, so transport dates often change. Since prison officials feared the date could be compromised, inmates could never really tell when the Gray Goose would pull up to take the inmates away.

Donnie had his few items ready. He vowed to spend the rest of his life reading and understanding the Bible and living in repentance. It was as if he was in a transitional period with God making him over and preparing him for Heaven.

About 9 p.m. two days later, five officers came to Donnie's cell and told him it was time to move out. Donnie and the other twenty inmates quietly got their things and put them in the plastic containers provided. They handed the containers to the officers and waved good-bye to their cells.

Donnie held his head down as the officers placed the shackles on. He had a few reasons to be sad. He had spent all his time served in this prison, with the exception of a little jail time he had to do before coming here – and the time in Mississippi. He, too, in some ways felt like he was home, being that Camden was only a few miles away. He felt connected with the marks on the walls made by the inmates who had died before him. In some strange way, Donnie wanted this to be the last building he would visit. He even thought of how he would miss the dingy smell of the old brick walls. Like most of the things in his life, the option to stay was out of his hands.

Donnie never cried in front of the officers, but since he would never see them again, shedding a tear was his last worry. As he turned towards the hall leading to the bus that would shuttle him away, he heard someone shout out.

"What the Flizz Zips Goenz Zon?"

As Donnie turned, there stood officer Miles, Donnie's manuscript in his hands, letting Donnie know that he received it. Because of what Officer Miles had yelled out, he knew that he must have read about six or seven chapters. He gave Officer Miles the thumbs up as he headed out the door. Officer Miles nodded and gave thumbs up in return.

As the prisoners got on the Gray Goose, Donnie looked back to see Elizabeth City State Prison for the last time. He sat with a glare in his eyes that would have penetrated steel.

Officer Miles, in fact, had been reading Donnie's manuscript, reading nonstop. He was amazed at the way Donnie was able to tell the story of his life and express himself in such detail. He also heard many inmates over the years talking about their innocence … but not Donnie. Donnie always talked about paying his debt to society.

As Officer Miles kept reading, he soon realized that Donnie's brother, Maurice, had killed those three women. Officer Miles understood that Maurice was responsible for the murders of Thai Simmons, Loretta Johnson, and China Gibbs. Officer Miles knew that **Three Lies** was exactly that … lies that Donnie had paid for and would pay for.

The only thing Donnie was responsible for was covering up for Maurice.

Officer Miles knew he would not be able to sleep knowing a murderer was still out there. He had trouble accepting that a man, though not entirely innocent, was about to be put to death for another man's crimes. Miles knew that he had to turn this manuscript over to the right authorities, but he wasn't sure just who. He didn't want it getting into the hands of someone that would cause him to lose control of it. He wanted to make good on his promise to Donnie that he would get it published.

Officer Miles could always count on Donnie to be straightforward with him. He did not want to contact Donnie and cause anymore suspicion because of all the problems he had when he worked on the Dead Hall. Miles had a family to take care of. He didn't want to get fired because of his actions on Donnie's behalf.

Miles also wanted to save Donnie's life, but he remembered Donnie saying that no matter what, he did not want his destiny altered. Officer Miles knew he had to keep his promise.

Donnie had left all kinds of clues in the book. All Miles had to do was go back and find them. He had to stop Maurice before someone else got hurt.

The first person he decided to contact was Beatrice Harold. All he wanted to do was see if she would allow him to speak with her about Donnie. Officer Miles was from New Land, a small town outside of Elizabeth City and about thirty-five miles from Camden. He had never been to Camden other than passing through on his way to the Outer Banks. From how Donnie described her in the story, she had to be a caring woman, Miles's thought.

When Officer Miles was off work one day, he decided to give Beatrice a visit. He got up early that morning and left for Camden. When he got a few miles from where Beatrice lived in Camden, he stopped this man riding a lawn mower on the main road.

"Excuse me, sir," Miles said politely, "could you tell me where I could find Beatrice Harold."

The man turned the mower off and faced Officer Miles to see who he was talking to. Officer Miles took one look at him and started to drive off because of how big the man's lips were. After all, he was driving a lawn mower on the highway.

"Excuse me," the man said, "are you talking to me?"

"Yes, could you tell me where Beatrice Harold lives?"

"You talking about old man Harry's old lady?"

Miles didn't know if that's who he was looking for or not, but it was a start. What were the chances of there being more than one Beatrice Harold in this small community, so Miles said, "Yes, that's her."

"Well, son, ya just keep on down this road til ya see a sign saying, Belcross. Ya make a right and go down 'bout four or five miles and then ya make a left on Pinch Gut Road. Make a left on North River Road. Second house on the right. And when you get there, tell her that Uncle Lips sent you. Ya got it, young fella?"

"Yes, thank you very much. And I'll tell her you sent me."

One thing about the country roads, they're long, but easy to find your way. Miles made it to Beatrice's house without a problem.

He pulled up in the yard and a beautiful twenty-something young lady came outside.

"Hi. I've been expecting you," she said. "My name is Beany. Will you please come in?"

As he walked into the house, there Beatrice was, sitting in the living room looking just as beautiful as the daughter.

"Yes, may I help you, sir?"

"Yes, ma'am."

"The name's Beatrice."

"Beatrice, Donnie wrote a book while he was at Elizabeth City State Prison, and he had a lot of information that led me to believe that he didn't commit those murders. He speaks of his brother as the killer and that he had no idea about any of them except the first one. He said that he only helped to cover it up. He also wrote that your daughter Beany communicated with him on several occasions. He also talks about you like he loved you more than his own mother. Not only in the book, but he talked about you to me whenever I was on watch. If there is anything you can tell me to help out, please feel free to do so."

Beatrice got quiet for a minute and then spoke.

"You know … those boys have been through to a lot. I tried to help them all I could, but I think they were just born with the mark. I never did think that Donnie had anything to do with the actual killings, but I didn't want to get too close to him because of that other boy."

"So, you are saying that you know that he didn't do these murders," Miles asked.

"My daughter has a gift, and she knows a lot of things. She told me that he didn't do them, but she could not say who did. Something about messing up the order of things."

"Yes, it would not have led you here to me," a soft, almost spirit-like voice said, as Beany came out of the kitchen. "You and Donnie were supposed to cross paths. You were supposed to inspire him to write this book. You were supposed to find me, and I am supposed to tell you the book is all true. Donnie left you clues in the book that will help set the blue birds free. Now, go. Go on your journey."

With that, Beany turned and walked back into the kitchen.

"You heard her! Now you just get to moving on out of here, young man. My heart can't take too much of this. I'm still trying to get used to all the backwater crap. Now, go on before I have a heart attack," Beatrice said.

As Officer Miles got back into his car, he noticed someone in a black raincoat, soaking wet, standing at the rear of the car. Whatever it was, it didn't look human. He hurried to get in the car, keeping his eyes on the person. After getting in the car, he quickly turned the ignition, put it in reverse, and looked out the rear-view mirror again. The person or thing he saw was gone. When he looked towards the front, he saw Beany walking back into the house. Officer Miles remembered Donnie saying how frightened he was of her, so he wasted no time getting out of the yard and on his way.

Once he was back on the road, he started to go over some of the things that he thought would be clues. Then it hit him. The man in the black coat. He remembered Donnie writing about seeing a man in a black coat when he was on the plane. He also thought about when Donnie said that Beany was standing at his door in a raincoat and hat when he was living with Beatrice. After what he thought he had just seen, he knew that was the key to the puzzle.

When Officer Miles got home, he asked his wife, Sandy, about the manuscript.

"I meant to ask you who wrote that, Stanley," she asked.

Officer Miles explained and she was stunned.

"He was a very sad man, wasn't he, honey?"

"I guess, when you think about it," Miles said. "How much of it did you read?"

"All of it."

"Do you remember anything about a man in a raincoat?"

"Yes! Scary, wasn't it? Especially the part about the letter Loretta wrote and the man standing out in the rain ringing her doorbell."

"That's it!" Miles shouted. "That's what I was looking for. Honey, get on the computer and look up every private detective agency in Norfolk. I got some work to do."

When Officer Miles found the private detective's number, he called him. He told him about the book and the murders. The detective agreed to meet with him and to take a look at the manuscript.

***

On June 7 at 12:01 a.m. Donnie was to be put to death. He was the first inmate to be put to death at the new wing at Central Prison. He was taken to an area where he received his last meal, which included an Andy's Cheesesteak, chilly fries, and a large pink lemonade.

Inside were two officers who would walk with him to the room where he was to be put to sleep. Also, in the room with Donnie for his last meal were Beatrice and Reverend McKnight. Beatrice remembered that when Donnie was a little boy, he never wanted to be by himself. She knew being with Donnie was the least she could do. She felt guilty for not attending his wedding or visiting him over the years. Donnie didn't seem to mind. He was just glad she was there.

Tavone was there for him spiritually and promised to be by his side to pray as they put him to sleep.

As he came closer to his death, Donnie started to write something he wanted to read before he died.

At 11:30 p.m. Donnie was escorted into the final room that would hold him behind the wires and brick walls. He was given the opportunity to speak with the Rev. McKnight. The warden gave Donnie a chance to make a final statement that would be available to the public afterwards. Donnie was lying there, knowing that behind the glass window was the witness room. He looked towards the window and began to recite the poem that he wrote just hours before:

***

Still

I cried too many times today ... and hurt badly inside

With no one to lean on ... I tried to stand ... alone

But I got lonely ... I always hated to be alone

Because of the empty feelings that continued to fill my heart

My heartbeat …

Became a silent reason to beat myself down

And down I went

Falling to the end of me …
And I hurt myself bad

With only a piece of life left in me

I began to pray
And I prayed hard … and long … and with
power …
And with the sincere tears of a broken man

With the unselfish shame of a beggar …
I gave my entire burden to Him
And, in return, He gave to me …
The calmness after a storm
The heartbeat of a thousand men
The rock to stand upon
The water to fill me …
The arms to hold me
And most of all … the love to love me
And now …

I will never lose the faith … knowing
In His arms … He will keep … me

God will keep me …

Still

***

After Donnie's last words, with tears rolling down his cheeks, he closed his eyes as he was informed by the warden that the execution had begun.

Beany and Beatrice set behind the class, tears pouring as they stared at Tavone wondering what part he had in this ending of a life. They knew that the long ride home in the pouring rain was going to be one for the ages.

As the five different syringes containing thiopental sodium, potassium chloride, pancuronium bromide, and a second dose of sodium pentothal pumped into his lifeline, they brought his existence to stillness.

As Donnie lay there as if he had fallen asleep, a mystic blue mist began to circle the room, lifting Donnie's soul from the stillness and flying him away.

None of the witnesses seemed to notice what was taking place, but for the crowd on the outside, it was a little different.

With candles and signs in their hands, the anti-death penalty groups stood outside the prison in their designated area. They didn't seem to mind the rain as it drenched the cold night. They continued to sing the traditional gospel hymns and chanted verses from the Bible.

The local TV news stations were there to report the time of death and any details they could get from the inside.

Then someone in the crowd pointed to a blue light they saw coming from the room where Donnie was put to sleep.

"It looked like something from the movie **Ghostbusters**," said a young boy, as the rest of the crowd looked on in awe.

"No, they are taking him home … the Blue Birds are taking him home," said Beany, in a ghost like figure, as her physical body set inside the execution with her eyes closed.

***

As Maurice watched the broadcast on the TV, he heard a knock on the door. He looked out his window to see who it was and wasn't surprised.

As rain fell like rocks off an overpass, Maurice watched as a man in a black raincoat and hat stood before his condo. He went back to his chair and sat there as if he didn't even notice the loud vicious knocks that soon followed.

Maurice continued to drink Jack Daniels as he watched Donnie's death repeatedly being reported on the news. He took his final drink straight from the bottle as the knocks at the door got even louder. Soon the knocks came with commands to open.

"Police! Open up. We need to talk with you about the murders of Thai Simmons, Loretta Johnson, and China Gibbs."

Maurice yelled to the officers.

"Come on in. My doors are always open."

As the police officers turned the doorknob and stepped in, they heard a loud report and advised the private detective to be careful. They pulled out their weapons and moved slowly through the small hallway leading into Maurice's living room. They quickly saw that Maurice could do them no harm.

As Maurice slouched in his chair with a self-inflicted bullet wound to the head, a dark shadow came over the room. The detective and officers watched as the shadow formed into a crow, went inside Maurice's body, and then passed through the window.

Private investigator Teddy Warden stood, his black raincoat and hat dripping puddles of water onto the carpet. He turned to the police officers and said, "Cripple cries make dancing lies, and I guess the truth came tonight."

"Just what does that mean?" a police officer asked. "I've heard a lot of old folks saying that."

Teddy looked at the body lying there.

"My old man used to say, the lies you hold inside will cripple you and cause you to dance with death. I guess Maurice could not live with the three lies Donnie died for ... and now Maurice's dance is over."

The End

KENT O' HUGHES

Black Frame:

Flight of the Blue Bird

Life-Inspired Poetry

INTRODUCTION

Nothing is purer than a child's heart. With that in mind, I began to work on a way to incorporate this thought into my next book of poetry. I first tested the idea on my daughter, Mia, who was two years old at the time. I asked her this question.

"What does it mean to be free?"

She quickly answered, "Lack uh boo burr" (like a blue bird).

After laughing for a few minutes at her wit, I began to think maybe she was on to something. I do not believe that things just happen. Being from the South, we always put things in order by the numbers, so here I go.

Number one: Why would I think to ask my baby a question about freedom?

Number two: How could she have given me such a perfect answer?

I often question myself, but never have I questioned God, so I began to look within myself for answers and for a way to make all of this work.

I began to visualize freedom and the price that we have to pay for it. At the end of the day, freedom isn't, and never was meant, to be free. And maybe, just maybe, neither are we. We are all slaves to **something,** to **someone,** or maybe even to **ourselves**. Allow me to give you a few examples of what I mean, so that you will not think I'm flying without wings.

If we work for the boss at a job where we'd rather not be and at the end of a pay period all our money goes to the things we love (i.e., mortgage, car payment, vacation or whatever), then we are in the category of a materialistic slave. *(Something)*

We, at some point, lived with our guardian, and we either did what that person said or, when the time was right, we left the nest. When we finally had our own pad, crib or apartment, we had to follow the landlord's rules in order to continue to occupy the space. Then we start a family. If we do the family thing right, we often may feel we want to change our name to Toby and chop off a foot to keep from running away. Staying is what I call becoming the responsibility slave. *(Someone)*

If you have ever wondered where your next meal was coming from, or how you'd buy your child's school clothes, or where you'd find your next job, or how you were going to keep your lights on and hold on to your house, and if you have ever wondered whether maybe you would be better off just flying the coop, you are what I call a mental slave. *(Ourselves)*

There are other ways of explaining this concept, like maybe talking about the state of the world.

War.

Fear.

Life.

Death and taxes.

These are the things that keep us locked inside the prison walls of our minds and bind us to do and think the unthinkable.

Trust me: If you put a little thought to it, you can think of things and situations that have caused you to not fly – things that caused you never to reach your greatest potential.

When I worked on my first project, you would not believe the many nay-sayers I encountered. It was if they were so negative, they had to have been born into slavery of the mind.

Using the word slavery loosely may seem a little reckless, but it's simple; you're either one or the other – a free person or a slave. Mentally, it's up to you.

Me.

I know I'm not free. Still, I choose to fly. "How?" you may ask.

Like a Blue Bird.

Your mind and your heart are two things that can take you as far away as you want to go. So when I think "freedom," it is with my eyes closed and with no caution. My flight starts with love and nourishment. How high I fly and how far I go depends on how deep my dreams are.

Always keep in mind the reality of darkness and the awesome power of light. The light will see you through.

Always look forward to the light.

CONTENTS

Frame One
The Love and Birth of the Blue Bird

In My Dreams
Untitled
If Love Had Eyes
Like The Tides
Love Like Us
Deep Breaths
4 U X 2
Last Time I Smiled
Always

Part 2
The Heartache of a Blue Bird

My Head, My Heart
Twisted Desires
Of Course You Won't
So Wrong
Yet
The Queen Of Dawn
How Do I Love Thee …

Frame Two
Flying in the Darkness

Part 1
The Death of a Blue Bird

Don't Unless

The Song of Flight
Life After My Death
Born To Die
Stand Up and Be Counted
Ashes

<u>Part 2</u>
<u>And From the Darkness to the Light</u>

Mad
Cup Of Tea
Rocks For Rent
Depression Kills
Dirty Other Brother
The Masses
Chains Still on Child

Frame Three
The Last Flight of the Blue Bird

The Last Flight of the Blue Bird

Focus On
Next Page
Gentle Creeks
Knowing
Keep Me Still
Brushed Smile

Misfits: The Bonus

Misfits Island
This Poem Stinks

What?
Blinded
Balancing The United
Self-Validation
Dance, Brother, Dance
What The Flizz Zips Goenz On
Lonely Monster
Haters Anthem
This Is My Second
Broken Frames of The Heart
Three Monsters Lived in A House
The Little Girl Who Sucked Her Thumb
Dream Like I Dream

KENT O' HUGHES

Frame One

The Love and Birth of the Blue Bird

The Love and Birth of the Blue Bird

In order to fly you must first break out of your shell, stretch your wings, not worry about what's out there, and just fly. You still seek nourishment from others, but once you have gained strength, growth, and confidence, you begin to wander away from the nest. Maybe not far at first, but eventually flight takes place.

After spreading our wings to fly, the first thing we seek is love and companionship.

So, the journey began.

The Love and Birth of the Blue Bird – the Black Frame way

In My Dream
Untitled
If Love Had Eyes
Like the Tides
Love Like Us
Deep Breaths
4 u x 2
The Last Time I Smile

In My Dreams

When time has cried
And the liquid sun
Has melted the rainbow skies

Forever stood beside me
Kissing away the hurt

Love ... began to softly pillow my dreams

Yet ... destroying my hopes

While ...

Reality captures visions of the truth
Releasing me from the wants

Yet ... pledging loyalty to my needs

With caramel tears I ...
Cried for you ...
To hold me
And hoped ...
Destiny will find time to dry my tears against
you ...
And lay its weary head upon my pillow
As I asked ... if only for one night

Forever to stand still – for us ...
And visions of the truth shown only
In my dreams

Untitled

Time passed through the chambers of multiform moons
Flashes of life's mystic drama are
overwhelmed by the beautiful memories.

Time passed through the chambers of multiform
moons
Life flashes, and mystic drama clears
the path for beautiful memories
My eyes blanket thoughts of you standing in
flowered fields
The sun kisses the ground as you step towards
me
Moving in slow motion
Your arms reach out as if to want me
Dying to comfort you
I stand ...
Heart beating with anticipation and disbelief
Until ...
We encircle with the passion
and warmth of a thousand loves
And
For one special moment time was kind ...
And
Understanding ...
And
Gentle
And.
Time ....
Was ours

KENT O' HUGHES

If Love Had Eyes

If love had eyes
It would see through and around me

It would see
How I was lost and how you found me

It would know
The colors of my unchanging heart

It would see
You to me and we would never part

If love had eyes
It would know how I feel

By the glow that shows
By the touch that's real

Understanding the magic
My love needs not to see

For if love had eyes
You would see love in me

Like The Tides

With every storm that passes
I imagine your brightness ...
Your candles ...
Lighting the darkest corners of my heart

Like the tides beating against the shores
I allowed your warmth
Your tenderness
To wash away my hurt and to ...
Cleanse my deep whispers of sorrow

With all that is to be ...
You are my shores ... I drift to you
And the sands of time will be our guide

Love Like Us

The physical moments
Your smile, my touch
Our embrace, our love
I need it so much
The time together
Our sweet good-byes
Our times, our moments
We cherish our cries
The way I'm feeling
Love must be true
For God made love
Then placed it in you

Deeps Breaths

Holding my breath,
      waiting to release what has been
      locked inside of me for years.
I've tried to listen to the music you've dance to

...

Many deep breaths I've inhaled
      to breathe the essence of you.
Lost in your direction ...
I move slowly, watching each step.
Measuring your song.
Singing in your key.
Unlocking my path to you
      and your unplaced melodies
I danced ... to the tune of your heart.
Thanking you for letting me live again,
And breathe again
Inside of you
And so deep.

4 U X 2

I live 4 u
Will die 4 u
Crawl
Walk
Run
Even fly 4 u

Never will I hurt
Or
Lie 2 u
If time brings u tears
I will cry 4 u

Ask me 2 jump
It's how high 4 u
If u want a pillow of clouds
I'll bring the sky 2 u
And if I can't find my way
I'll still get by 4 u

If u decide I failed
I'll still try 4 u

I am blue bird in love

I won't hide it from u
I will love u 4 ever
And times that by 2

The Last Time I Smiled...

It was because of you
I thought about all the times
    you told me how special I am
    and how I made you feel more hold
I remember when my world was crumbling
I stood before you
Holding back my tears
As my voice cried out to you
The warmth and calmness of your words
comforted me
    Your actions validated my existence
    And for that...
    I love you
The last time I smiled
I thought of my need to hug and kiss you
And how you would embrace me gently
But...
Like all things given unto us
A part of your heart
You shared with me
I remember thinking how it how it would be for
us to be together again
    Sweet thought
    Then I just smiled...again
    The last time
    I thought about our dreams
    And how you helped them come true
    It's funny how time catches hold like a big wind
and blows life right by you
    If I could place time in a bottle...

I would take memories of us and turn them
upside down each hour just to relive them…
Funny thought…then I smiled
The last time I smiled
It was because you

Always

She said…

When my arms don't seem long enough to
reach,
    know that my heart is holding you.
    When my lips are not close by,
    know the words I speak
    Moisten all your imagination.
    When you don't see me,
    know that I am always there!

And when time has placed
the blessings that we pray for
in front of us to grasp,
Let us make sure that we take full advantage
of…
    Each other's presence's
    and use our time to measure our gift (our love).

And He said…

Your love for me,
Are the arms that reaches out to me,
Your lips hold the smile I smile with.
In you I found the lost me and you too must
know that…
    I am always there!

ALWAYS

Part 2
The Heartache of a Blue Bird

After we find what we seek to be the truth in love, we begin to DO anything in the name of love.

The poem "4 u x 2" sounds just a little bit too desperate, it seems, but sacrifice is one of the most important ways to show honor and commitment in love. Most of the verbs used to explain our deepest feeling towards each other can be used as fuel when the wall of love comes tumbling down.

Sacrifice becomes ... after all I've done for you and that's the thanks I get

Honor becomes ... I hate your guts

Cherish becomes ... I'm leaving

And Commitment becomes ... I want what's mine plus half of yours.

After the blue bird begins its downward fall, which can be a lonely one, the Heartache of the Blue Bird starts ... the Black Frame way, of course.

My Head, My Heart
Twisted Desires
Of Course You Won't
So Wrong
Yet
The Queen of Dawn

My Head, My Heart

My head tells me I should let you go
My heart starts to plead, crying out hell no

My eyes show my feelings what I need to see
My   feeling   gets   in   the   way   of   my
responsibilities

My love for you is deeper than hell's bottomless
pit
Yet my head tells my heart not to fall for that
shit

I see you in my dreams
I taste you in my mouth
Yet ... when I awake, I'm spitting nightmares
out

My heart keeps wondering back
To the days when we were strong
Yet my head always reminds me of ...
How this love was so wrong

And if I ever be in a position where I find you in
my bed
Just keep playing with my heart while I'm using
my head

Twisted Desires

Twisted desires
Burning blood
The bottom of loneliness

Too much sugar
In your coffee
Brain swollen from the stress

Spit from Satan's cup as ...
You're lying straight up
You're in lust
With infested tears

You've been dying to love
But you don't know how
Been in lust for so many years

As Satan's group gathers
To push you in
Your heart fights back
But your head never wins

When new blisters form
Your cracked skin burns
You talk to yourself
You never learn

Oil from the midnight
Softens your cracks
But ... too late for I'm sorry
There is no turning back

Your shit hit the fan
And blew back in your face
Your twisted desire
Left you ...
In a twisted state

Of Course You Won't

Your bone chilling smile
Only weakens my knees
Your warm weather walks
Makes sweat just bead
From my forehead to my ankles
It's you that I need

Now ...
I beg of you ...
Please ...

Don't tease me with your silky cream voice
Don't touch me right there
It makes me moist
The words you whispered
Are my words of choice?

Now ... I beg you to keep me on course

But of course, you won't listen
And you'll entertain my thoughts
And won't be satisfied
Until us both get caught
And the lesson we learn
Isn't worth the lesson being taught

Sometimes ... I can't believe that I bought

Into the fact
That I was meant for you
It's that you're so damn ... damn

It just had to be true
But of course you aren't
And of course you knew
So right now ... it's ... the hell with you

So Wrong

Lying beneath the short breaths you took
As you frantically begged for more
I ...
Wondered in and of this mixed passion
Enjoying the warmth of your body
Yet trembling with the reckless excitement of ...

KNOWING ...
I AM SO WRONG

YOU SEE ...

I've held you tighter
Even with more passion
Even more times than I can remember ...

In my dreams

But to live this fantasy

This dream comes true

Defines life as it's meant to be

Now ... that you're in the flesh
The reality of us together now weighs heavily
on my conscious
Indeed I must please you
Yet ... self-fulfillment distracts my every effort

So I began to ...

Measure each timely stroke
Until I lost time and began to rabbit each
movement
And each pelvic thrust
And each thrust was one of jubilation
And each grunt meaningful and a serious
movement
Until I could no longer control myself

And in seconds it was over

Hell! Less than sixty

I began to explain ...

I don't what happened

I can't explain

This is the first time this has happened

I just wanted you so bad

I can't explain it

Lying beneath the short breaths you took ...
You frantically whispered ...

Only in your dreams will you
        ever waste another of my minutes ...

Man!

KNOWING …
SHE WAS SO WRONG

Yet

You kill me softly
Yet I refuse to die

Your tears confuse me
Yet you vowed not to cry

Your razor-sharp words
Cut through me like glass

You complain today
Like we live in the past

When I'm with you
You're not
At least that's how I feel

Yet, you want me to act
And pretend that it's real

It's a shame
I'd rather be alone
Than to ever be with you

Yet leaving you is something
I just can't do

The Queen of Dawn

The Queen of Dawn
Kiss my thoughts
And turn me left
Where love was taught

I learned to love
And lost all time
When the love she gave
Wasn't even mine

With one sweet whisper
I flipped the rolls
To shatter the truth
That's yet untold

I wipe the smile
Off Dawn's sweet face
And the tears I cried
Were soon replaced

With morning sun
And evening rain
A brand-new lover
Screwed my brain

And where she thought
She had me fooled
I took her young ass back to school

Now the Queen of Dawn
She claimed to be

KENT O' HUGHES

Was the Queen that made
A King of me

How Do I Love Thee...
Let Me Check My Blood Pressure

I placed my hands on my heart today just to check if I
was alive
I detected a beat and realize I was more than alive
I was also in motion
I moved like the winds
Silent and calm yet with reason and a destiny
You see...
My winds, for some reason, keep leading me to you
I prayed that we didn't blow our moment... like a bad
storm
And I hope like a leaf that floats on the wings of the
wind
We land in each other's arms
For...
Like all that is warm in my heart
And all that beats within
You make me feel more alive when I think of you
You are my summer breeze and...
You simply warm my heart
But tomorrow I will hate you all over

And have to check my Blood Pressure...again

Frame 2

Flying in the Darkness

Part 1
The Death of a Blue Bird

Sometimes during flight, we tend to rest our wings. Life begins to spiral downward, and we start to question ourselves. Maybe at some point we even question "why fly" in the first place. With few doubts and many disappointments, we find a comfort zone. I'll call that zone "the darkness."

As much as we hate to admit it, we have all visited this place at least once in our lives, if only for a minute. Whether we seek counseling, prayer, and some other method or quick fix, we've all been there.

I was once in a class where the instructor asked, "How many of you have ever thought about death, or maybe at some point wished, said, or thought to yourself that maybe you'd be better off dead."

Everyone in the class looked around at each other with no one raising a hand. Now know that I, in the privacy of my own little box, may have said or thought about it at some point, but quickly came up with a million reasons to live, one being, "Who's going to take out the trash tomorrow?"

Fearing I may have been the only one to cross that bridge, I wasn't about to say anything, so I just sat there quietly. Needless to say, we all found that at some point, death has crossed all our minds via television, loss of a loved one, or maybe just wondering what's next after this. One way the instructor put it was, if we watch the news and hear of a murder, we may say something like:

It's a shame that she had to die like that.

It's not fair.

He was too young.
It must have been her time.
If you find me dead, I don't care what the note says: Please investigate because whoever did it ... it wasn't me.

All these reactions, she said, are normal human responses, yet it proves that at some point it must have crossed each person's mind. You see, I would like to go when I'm about one hundred years old, in my sleep, after a wild night of sex, and when it's my time. How about you?
Here are some delusions of grandeur to ponder.
The Death Sentences... the Black Frame poetry way.

Don't Unless
The Song of Flight
Life After My Death
Born to Die
Fight, Win or Die
Stand Up and Be Counted
Ashes

Don't Unless

Don't bring a flower to my grave
Unless you're celebrating my life
Don't volunteer any answers
To any questions I had
Unless you know they're right

Don't smile in my face
Unless you're really happy
Even then, don't smile too much
Don't hold out your hand
Unless you are wearing gloves
I'm resting … don't want to be touched

Bring no whiskey to my party
Unless it's you doing the drinking
Don't spend too much time
Doing a lot of talking
Unless you've really done some thinking

Don't tell anyone that you knew me
Unless you know my brother's name
Even then don't say it too loudly
Don't want you putting my family to shame

Don't dress me up in a new suit
Unless it's the one I bought
I don't want some stranger to dig me up
Or give people something to talk about

Just send me off with maybe a tear
To show how much you cared

And you will understand
Like ...
I understood
And we'll talk when I meet you there

The Song of Flight

Clip the wings of a blue bird
Now listen to the song he sings
As beautiful as the ocean blue
Or soft taps from the rain

The song could be from sorrow
Knowing he may never fly again
Maybe it's a song of joy and delight
Or he's calling of a friend

It could be he sings about the past
And how he used to soar so high
If you listen closely and imagine this ...
The song ... could be a cry

Imagine ...

Hugging a rainbow on a clear blue day
Or kissing the clouds as they pass your way
One clip, no wings
He's singing beautifully they say
or
WAS THE BLUE BIRD TRYING TO PRAY?

Life After My Death

I question my mortality
My life after ... my death
A few puffs of smoke
To clog my path
And shorten my every breath

Feeling like my distant past
Wasn't always what it seemed
My life after my living for self
My nightmare after my dream

Coughing up reality
Spitting out hopes and fears
Smiling while I'm crying
Yet I keep on trying
Been dying many years

Struggling with my future

Lost in darkness

Constancy pulls to the other side

Walking backwards to my destination
Wanting to run and hide

I close my eyes to light my path
And watch as they come for me

Place behind me ...

The angels of mercy
Someone must watch over me

I tried to shake him off my back
But he manages to reach the top
The angels of mercy soon flew away

Please stay and make him stop

Now I am closer to the answer
My life after death has come
And I no longer question my mortality

I only question where I'm from

Born To Die

Fourteen carrots

Dingy grins

Dark shadows
As I awake

Lonely walls

Tears that fall
Why will thou forsake

Too many nothings
Fill my heart
Dirty pillow I do hold

Aching smile

The killer child

My grief be the story told

Nasty memories

Faded hope

Trying to replace the hate

Once all trash
My dreams burned like cash
Why will thou forsake

Losing reality

Gaining emptiness

Filled with anger
But Why

My chances were slim
Once I knew Him
'Cause like Him, I was born to die

Stand Up and Be Counted

Weary eyes and abandoned dreams
Detached the moments of hope
Reality set
Memories met
Dark clouds and skies elope

Take the blue birds

Weaken their souls
And proclaim you made them strong
Rebuild your solid masterpiece
And hope it lasts for long

Twisted tales
Passed through the tube
Computed by ignorant minds
Believe the scene
True stories untold
The truth is hard to find

Explained by the powers
Small words used
To embrace the senseless fight
United we stand
We stand right now
We kneel
And pray by night

Cut down the middle
Pull the plug
And see what you have done

The autopsy shows
How the east winds blow
And how the war has just begun

Lay down your illusions
Your brick walls of confusions
And crush the stereotype
Or Death to us all when the curtains fall

And we died with all our might

Ashes

Ashes in his drops
Mud puddles at his feet
Rusty colored memories
So raw that they can't sleep

Dark clouds cover his coffin
As laid next to the dirty man
The control of the sons of the mother
Trigger finger detached from his hands

Sour drops of mercy
Explain his nasty eyes
Staring at the feet of the hungry
Turning the truth into lies

At the belly of the scorpion
Acid burns through his skin
Sickening thoughts of the murdered man
Who was trying his best to win?

Each notch represents his madness
So proud that he salutes
They took him down
That hot damn clowns
Love had no substitutes

Crawl back into your thorns
You are killing all of us
Who figured you would pull the trigger
You know in God we trust

You are not
So don't get too happy
Don't dig flowers from the Far East
Why crash the songs of the blue birds
And kill the world of peace

Awaken by the storms
And pulling the wrinkles from his face
He understood he was sleeping
So he faded back to that place

Were nightmares of self-destruction
Allow the blue eyes to reprimand the brown
Snake-bitten words used to build his temples
Eager to bring them down

He cried knowing they were coming
And knowing he would die soon enough
He allowed us into his gates of hell
Just to prove that he was tough

With ashes in his tear drops
And mud puddles at his feet
When he awakens from his nightmares
They'll put his ass to sleep

Part 2
And From the Darkness to the Light

In Part One of this frame, I went where no man likes to go. At some point it can consume us all, if we let it. I know that I'm not ready to meet with Mr. Death ... just yet.

How about you?

Many people are scared to go beyond the box. But if you ever want to control your destiny, you must seek the truth in each meaning and study the script that has been written for you.

Some choose to watch the news, sit back ... and wait for the world to blow up.

I learned a long time ago that you will never change the world. Changing the world means changing people.

The thing you can do is ... make the world better by becoming a better person.

You will never be able to solve everyone's problems, nor will you be able to solve all of yours. But we all know that the first step in problem solving is to identify the problem. No matter the conclusion, you must continue to fly until God decides to clip your wings. And when that time comes, you will have flown with the best of them, and you will fly From the Darkness to the Light ... the Black Frame way.

Mad
Cup of Tea
Rocks for Rent
Depression Kills
Dirty Other Brother

The Masses
Chains Still on Child

Mad

Mad with the world
So I swing at the wind
Mentally attacking
The hatred within
Brutally striking
The inner-made man
Bruised was the deck that was place in my hand

Sick of the right wing
Tired of the left
Ill with the world
So I'm mad with myself
Mad with the fool
That borrowed my time
Or was I the fool thinking the world was mine?

Dead ...
Are the memories
That hang around?
Alive ...
Are the demons?
Can't keep the down
For every time I place myself
Out of the box
I start to catch heat when the kitchen gets hot

Burned ...
By society
My conscious was softened
Tear drops on my pillow
Blood stains on my coffin

The inner me talks
With a subliminal twist
Emotionally caught up in a subconscious bliss

The medication kicks in
And I'm out for the count
And the world ain't changed a bit
So tomorrow I'll swing
At the four winds that blow

Understanding that it won't change shit

Cup Of Tea

Next door lives a memory
I visit it each day
It invites me for a cup of tea
It begs for me to stay

It forces me to share the pain
It takes me by the hand
Why I keep going back there
I can't quite understand

Part of me ....
Can't bare the suffering
The other part
Can't stand the tears
Each day I pray
For it to go away
Though it's been here so many years

Its disguise is so beautiful
It dances in my sorrow
When it invites me back
I decline
Knowing I'll be back tomorrow

Next door there lives a memory
A memory that needs a friend
But the last cup
Damn near killed me
So the visits had to end

Rocks For Rent

Paper cuts

Brushes with death

Blinded by the light

Cripple cries

Dancing lies

The truth shall come to light

Dead man sick

Dusty coughs

Bleeding brick walls stand fast

Your mind's all bent

Selling rocks
For rent

To break your mom's heart of glass

Cats barking at the moon

Good morning

It's dinnertime

Found what you were looking for
And then you lose your mind

Killer weed

Brushes with death

Dizzy from the smoke

Laughing madly
Funeral's today

And life was just a joke

There you sat

Reality hit

And you're back inside yourself

The funny thing is ain't nothing changed
And you wish you had never left

Depression Kills

In silence I sit

In pitch black
I see

The storms of life
Umbrella me

Rejection fades
My rays of light

I'm that blue bird singing

The song of his life

Misery and mystery
Befriended me
Salvaging my straps
Very angrily

THREE KNOCKS ON THE DOOR
DEAFEN MY EARS
TWO WITH SERIOUS ANSWERS
ONE WITH FAKE TEARS

Behind the glass door
I saw through my pain

My storms of life
Withstood the rain

Difficult hurdles
Were met with hope
But when I asked me did, I love me
My answer was … Nope

So there I sat

With death in my eyes

Believing myself

Trusting my lies

Once filled self-hatred
And nonstop tears

Emotionally disturbed

DEPRESSION KILLS

Dirty Other Brother

When the simple things seem so complex
You kneel to pray and prepare for what's next
You throw up your guards
But get no respect

So you shield off the good in you

It's those
Dirty other brothers
That's holding you down
Because of the other dirty brothers
That they hang around
And when you throw your guards up
You get beat to the ground

So you shield off the good in you

Now ...
Someone once told you
That you were a star
Me ...
I agree because I think you are
It's those dirty other brothers
That pushed you too far

So you shield off the good in you

Until ...
That morning you open your eyes
And like Maya Angelou
You said ... I rise

And when you faced those other brothers
You caught them by surprise

And you kick those thoughts of
    other brothers to the side

At the top of your game
You couldn't be touched
The problem was ...
You missed those other brothers too much
It's like you had two broken legs
And they were carrying your crutches

Still, you kept them other brothers at bay

In the midst of the night
Those other brothers come a-creeping
And you had one eye
When they thought you were sleeping
They kept a-coming, and you kept a-keeping

All those dirty other brothers away

    You managed to keep those other brothers in the
dark
    And found their bites weren't half as bad as
their bark
    And you made it was as simple as a walk in the
park
    When you learned to follow your heart

The morale of this story is simply fact
If you take one step forward those

      other brothers will hold you back …
But it's got to be you to carry
        your own damned slack and remember
…
All those other brothers ain't black

The Masses

Formed by the masses
Then they place us in classes
Then pick us out one by one
They did today what y'all did yesterday
And yet nothing seems to get done

You create little monsters
Caged their minds
And expect them to follow the book
They can't read a lick
So you use the stick
To measure how long it took

Misrepresentation potted the seed
To raise the brows of a nation
They did what you let them
Now you want God to help them
When it's part of your creation

Your mangled conception
Allowed you to blame
Race and religion
For what you have done

But no tears in our eyes
For it's your time to cry
And again, the masses have won

Chains Still on Child

Tested by time
An evolution of dreams
Castaways depart …
On silent beams
By daylight …
Shine
By night …
Unseen
No future, yet told
Only death it seems

Deep beneath the halls of pains
Link together by balls and chains
Tremendous …
Spirit
Nothing to gain
Only sad memories
Of guilt and shame

Called upon
By mercy and grace
The heels of dawn …
Were soon replaced …
By trembling hills …
Devouring old faces

Still …

My secrets rest …
Within these places
Hidden behind my secret smiles

My future …
Untold …

Chains Still on Child

Frame 3

The Last Flight of the Blue Bird

The Last Flight of the Blue Bird

When you have traveled the unpaved roads of life and met each stumbling block with careful steps, a changing of the guard leads you to wisdom and understanding. All that is left for you to do is prepare for your final destination. You now understand just how strong you are after defeating the monsters of despair and greeting the friendly smiles of hope.

Set before you were the elements of choice and decisions. With the wisdom of a thousand kings, you boldly went where no man has ever gone before.

You went on your journey.

At some point, when the elements of life are in line, each of us becomes whole with self and finds that the real meaning of life is to eat, drink, be merry and multiply – not necessarily in that order.

I've learned one thing about life and love: You must live each day to the fullest and no matter what hand you are dealt, you must love yourself first and, in return, you will find it easy to love others.

Remember: the last flight of the blue bird can be a lonely one if you let life fly by without ever catching the winds. The last flight of the blue bird is the flight that returns you to love, strength, and understanding – the Black Frame way.

Focus On
Next Page
Gentle Creeks
Knowing
Keep Me Still
Brushed Smile
Just a lil dab a do ya

Focus On

Clearing my path
Understanding my journey
Focusing on my destination
A dark cloud may form to distract my norm
But it only fuels my determination

No mountains

No rocks

No signs or roadblocks

Can knock me off my course
Failure isn't written in my stones
I'm thinking failure is only a matter of choice
Flooded potholes may scatter my highway
Or
A smoother paved road may be on the right
Of the one I follow

I will live with tomorrow
So I walk with the angels by night
Crawl through the mud if I have to crawl
Stand in the rain if I must
But what I my not do
Is believe in you
For only in God I trust

Next Page

Watch me unfold
Don't believe what you're told
Get to know me and I'll only get better
Don't judge me by my skin
Because deeper ... within
I'm the force behind each word and each letter
Simple as I may speak
Within I am deep
My smile won't subsurface my thoughts
But in a quick minute
I'll dig right in it
And amaze you the vision I've caught
I see things with great eyes
Separating the truth from the lies
Smelling trouble from a mile away
Turn the next page and you are frozen on stage
Mesmerized by the words that I say
I don't hold out my hand
Nor do I need pats on my back
To confirm
Whether I'm on or off track
Believing in a higher being
I search for the truth in each meaning
And ...
My mother ... **SHE** ...taught me that

Gentle Creeks

Lost among the gentle creeks
That flow through your times in life
A rock or two may block your view
As determination boosts your stride

Destination peels the faded paint
And your true colors are showing
You get an uplift as you follow the drift
When the winds of life are blowing

As you paddle up creek fighting the flow
Determined to go against the grain
You find your way
When your clouds are gray
On your darkest hour
You withstood the rain

On your final call you understood it all
And you found your pot of gold
Lost among the gentle creeks of life
Where all calm waters flow

Knowing

Castrated memories
Distraught dreams
Formulated by sorrow and tears
The physical evidence
Displayed ... pain inside
You've suffered so many years

Lost in darkness
Blinded by hopelessness
That reflected your rays of light
Interwoven are the sprinkles from heaven
To pillow your tears at night

Trouble used to follow
Your every movement
Sweet sensitive steps you take
Knowing the eyes of God are watching you
And He makes no mistakes

You forgot what had passed you
Trouble won't last you
Respected are your ways of new
So you counted your blessings
With the miracle of the lessons
For in the morning your troubles are few

Keep Me Still

I cried to many times today ...
       and I hurt so much inside.
With no one to lean on ...
       I tried to stand-alone
But I got lonely
Because of the empty feelings
       that continued to fill my heart
My heartbeat ...
Became a silent reason to beat myself down
So down I went
Falling to the end of me ...
And I hurt myself so bad

With only a piece of life left in me

I began to pray
And I prayed hard ... and long
I prayed with power ...
And with the sincere tears of a broken man
With the unselfish shame of a beggar
       I gave my entire burden unto Him
And, in return, He simply gave unto me
The calmness of an after storm
The heartbeat of a thousand men
The rock to stand
The water to fill me
The love to love me
And the arms to make me hold
Never will I lose the faith
Knowing in His arms ...
He will forever ...

Keep me …
God will …
Keep me still …

Brushed Smiled

This morning ...
The sun
Slapped me in the face like a palmed hand on a
wet ass.
Being the recipient of this rude awakening
I demanded that the sun
Give into the darkness
Allow me to play fetus
And ...
Curl up into the warmth of my covers
And come out only after
I've dilated ten centimeters and was ready
to face this so called
Cold
Cold
Calculating
World

Knowing the brutal attack of tomorrow
Because of my action this morning
I crawled out of bed with the pace
of a dew-winged fly with a broken leg.
After making my way into my rebirthing
chamber
where the warmth of the control tapping waters
Washed off the old.
As I dried off the old flesh
and
Placed on the new
Which
I had placed out the night before,

I then wiped the fog off my reflection
Looked into the mirror and began
to sing my morning ritual:
Brown skin – Good morning – Brown skin
I don't know how your day's going to begin
and I can't tell you how …
your day is going to end …
and then …
The watch started tick-in
And I began to … brush my smile
I …
Brushed …
My …
SMILE …
And what a beautiful smile it was
Well …
Maybe to me and my mother

I then got my things and headed out into that
Cold
Cold
Calculating
World
Where I was greeted with a …
Foot in the ass
A stab in the back
And a …
"Good morning, Mr. Hughes"
Yes!
A
Brushed
Freaking
SMILE

Just a lil dab a do ya

It doesn't take that much from me… if you want to see me shine
Don't have to share my love with you…
Simple…
Because what's yours… is mind
If you decided that you failed
Don't let your rainy-day fool ya
All you need is lil sunshine from me…because...

Just a lil dab a do ya!

I could buy you that bike, that car, or that truck…
for you to get here if you can
Don't really need to reduce the temperature …
Because babe, I'm the man…and
If you decided that you're interested
Come and let me school ya
All you need is one lil bit of me…because

Just a lil dab a do ya!

Lotions are water based
Creams have natural blends
I'll rub you in the fineness of oils…if you just let me in
But nothing really can compare
And nothing more exciting or truer
Than the skills I have with these hands…remember

Just a lil dab a do ya

MISFITS:

The Bonus

Misfits Island

What would Black Frame be without a misfit frame?

I always seem to come up with a few poems that I can't put with the rest. These are the ones I come with right after I think I'm finished with my book. Some are funny and some seem to make no sense at all or have but little meaning. I think leaving them out just because one may **STINK** would be an injustice. Again, I placed them on their own little island. I guess you could say they are the special ones.

Being that my girls are the most important creatures on this earth to me, I wanted to share their talents with the world. Kenesha, 18; Chasity, 6; and Tamia, 3, allowed me to share their work with you.

I'd like to welcome you to Misfits Island.

This Poems Stinks

This poem is going to smell like …
Your daddy's feet on the coffee table
    After he takes off his three-year-old
work boots
It's going to smell
Like a tobacco field sprayed with hog waste
    on the hottest day of the summer
    and the wind is blowing your way …
It's gonna stink …
Like a dead mouse inside the walls of your
living room
    Like weed and alcohol breath
    in the morning after smoking a cigarette
This poem is going smell like Florida
    after President Bush was elected …
    something smells fishy
Like a nasty divorce
Like THE … N-word … not my word of choice
Like a fart blowing off course …
    and you think it went in your mouth….
This is going to smell
Like the middle of your underwear
Like the rear end of a polar bear
Like restroom at a gas station
This is going to smell
    like … music without a good beat
Like not voting but complaining about the
country

Like terrorism

266

Yes… this poems stinks like that …
And it will continue to smell until
        we wake up and smell what the world is
cooking.

What?

Open
Shut

My work is done
I played your game
I lost, you won

Happy
Sad

My emotions were strong
You broke me down
It didn't take long

Fast
Slow

That's how time went
You slept on me
And paid no rent

Believe
Doubt

The difference is clear
I distanced myself
When you came near

Up
Down

I reached the top
But soon I fell
I could not stop

Left
Right

Which way did I go
I lost myself
And did not know

Back
Forth

I could not choose
You played to win
I played to lose

Right
Wrong

I did not care
Where you were
When I needed you there

Empty
Full

My cup overflowed
But soon it cracked
From an overload

Open

KENT O' HUGHES

Shut

No smiles on my face
Courts adjourned
I rest my case

Blinded

I isolated my dreams from reality
Then placed myself on hold
I listened to each word she said
But believed not one word told
I counted the times she broke my heart
And divided them by her smile
I wanted to touch a piece of heaven with her
But begging just wasn't my style
Whenever I needed her warm embrace
Lukewarm was all she gave
Bonded by her grace and beauty
My flesh became my slave
Only when she needed money
Did she tease me with her love
She made it all feel so good
Like sunshine sent from above
Until one day she found anew
Did I realize what she had done
I isolated my dreams from reality
I played her game and won

Balancing The United

Two worlds in one
Divided we stand
Strong as ever
Our might comes
With our freedom

Even in our struggles
We stand strong
Wanting the same
Having separate yet equal dreams
Dying for our cause
Living …
To stop dying for our cause

The pot is melting
The ingredients are stirred
With misunderstanding
Distrust and biases
Yet we will brag
Brag that we are all that's right with the world
After all, …
We are two worlds

Divided we stand
United we fall

It's all about the balance

Self-Validation

His body was his temple
His soul belongs to heaven
His innocence was his gift
But was taken away by seven

In silence he cried for mother
In his room he begged him to stop
At school he would shy away
He kept his secrets on lock

A sea of anger molded him
And built a monster by age ten
The abuse had gotten worse
And he started to die within

No one knew what happened
So much he needed to share
Yet he kept this all a secret
He felt like no one cared

By his teens he began to search
But his silence kept him trapped
His pain became his reasoning
Until one day he just snapped

Others felt his pain
He crushed all that was in his path
His mother started to question his actions
He just looked at her and asked:

"Where were you when he did this?

"Why didn't you listen to me?
"Why did I have to be the apple
"That fell so far from the tree?
"Why didn't you have the courage?
"Why didn't you make him stop?
"Don't pretend you didn't notice
"When he stepped outside of his box."

As time passed, he reached out for help
He found it wasn't his fault
He found what happened to him
Didn't define what he had thought

Although the pain never truly stopped
He found he was at his best
When he learned of self-validation
And let God burden the rest

Dance, Brother, Dance

Death passed me by
Smiled and said
You have my mark
Upon your head
Just keep playing my
Dark-ass games
Keep your elders crying
When they hear your name

Follow my music
Love my beat
My shoes were made to fit your feet

Dance, brother, dance
Show me your heart
Don't let these saints tear us apart

Death passed me by
And left a trail
I blindly followed
But could not tell
By the way I followed
So willingly
The way I was living
Was killing me

Until I snatched me
From death's dusty hands
Dying was the child
I called …
A man

Never seeing passed my own demise
Truth in the tears
Death in the lies

To right my wrongs
I must set me free
And enjoy the life
God has given to me

What The Flizz Zips Goenz On

Why does my grandfather pay so much for his medication?

And when he prays, why is it always out of desperation?

Why do our kids think it's un-cool to get an education

And why do they always prepare themselves for incarceration?

With no tears coming from their eyes ...
    tell me ... what's their motivation...

Listen...

Why do so many fathers run away from child support?

And why are they so hard on the father who tries to do his part?

Why do mothers scream foul play, but won't show up in court

And why is the child the one's who left with the broken heart?

Tell me...

Why can't we all pay more attention to our government

And why can't we all live rent free like the president?

Why, even with land and a home, I can't get money lent?

Why two days after payday my money's already
spent?

Tell me…

What the flizz zips goenz on?
What the flizz zips goenz on?
What the flizz zips goenz on?
What's going on?
What's going on?

Lonely Monster

Refusing to let the lonely monster
Rear its ugly head
Trying to help the peace resurfaced
To fill this empty bed
Long nights reveal the darkest moons
That cradle me slowly to sleep
Caught up in a mental state
My pillow bears thoughts too deep

In the midst of this brainstorm
I found a ray of light
Calling on the blessings of so many
To replace the shadows of night
I sat behind the walls of pain
That blocked myself from me
It's easy once I understood
What will be …will simply be

Haters Anthem

You stood and watched
As I went into action
You wanted me to fail
With no satisfaction
You sat beside me
Looking over my shoulder
I performed my task
While you got even bolder
You said that ... all I try
Will fail

This is My Second

I could not tell
The end results
Was a passing grade
I built my house
With the bricks you laid
Your criticism ... no doubt...
Made me strong
You didn't believe
You don't belong
The next time you decide
To open your trap
Just read this poem
And consider it a slap

Broken Frame of The Heart
(By my eighteen-year-old daughter, Kenesha Hughes)

A picture fell today
broken glass spread across the floor
I cut myself picking up pieces
the pain is irrelevant.
I focus more on the picture of us.
We were happy then…
In Love.
Now…
I feel like that frame,
broken into little pieces.
Again…
I would hurt myself,
trying to pick US back up,
like the frame.
I can replace…the frame,
five dollars or less.
But the smile,
The smile that once embraced my face,
can no longer shine
for that smile turned into
broken images of the heart.

Like shattered glass.

Like…

A broken Frame of the Heart

Three Monsters Lived in A House
(By my six-year-old daughter, Chasity Hughes)

Three monsters lived in a house.
One monster kicks.
One monster spits.
One monster didn't do anything.
The monster who kicks name was Grumpy.
The monster that spits name was Grimish.
The monster that doesn't do all that name was Ben.
One day they went downtown. Everybody looked at them and they ran back to their house.
All they wanted was some ice cream. The people ran because they didn't like monsters.
The monsters were sad because the people ran from them.
They decided to share, play and make friends with the town's people.
Grimish shared lollipops. Grumpy took turns riding bikes, and Ben played with them.
That made the people happy.
The monsters went back home happy. Grimish and Grumpy spit and kicked. Ben didn't do all of that.

The End

The Little Girl Who Sucked Her Thumb
(By my three-year-old daughter, Tamaia Hughes)

One little girl sucked her thumb, and her name was Barbie. She kept sucking her thumb and her thumb fell off. It went on the ground, and it was nasty. Then she played on the computer.

The End

Dream Like I Dream
(A letter to the reader)

When you dream like I dream
You dream in color
Not only do you vision it
You ...
Taste
Touch
Embrace
And feel it
You hold onto it like you would a newborn
You nourish it
Pray and claim it

When you dream like I dream
You dream with a passion
Not only enthused with it
You trust
Believe
And know it
You share it with others like you would
        any other good fortune

When you dream like I dream

Whatever you dream will come true
Just imagine
You are living that dream
It takes more than a dream to make it come true
It takes you working at that dream
And God to make it a reality
If you dream like I dream

ABOUT THE AUTHOR

Kent Hughes is a native of Camden, North Carolina. He spent nine years in the United States Army as an infantryman and is currently works and lives in Raleigh with his wife.

His hope is to inspire one if not all, to follow him into a world where everything can be exactly the way you want it to be ... if you capture your imagination and bind it in your own book. Thank you for reading and see you on Pinchgut Road!!